PERFECT

Summer

kailin gow

A New Adult/Contemporary Adult Loving

Summer Novel

Perfect Summer (Loving Summer #2)

Perfect Summer

Published by THE EDGE

THE EDGE is an imprint of Sparklesoup Inc.

Copyright © 2013 Kailin Gow

For information, please contact:

THE EDGE at Sparklesoup

1·252 Culver Dr., A732

Irvine, CA 92604

www.sparklesoup.com

First Edition.

Printed in the United States of America.

ISBN: 9781597480567

Prologue

I know that whatever you decide, you'll be happy, Summer, and that is the only thing I could ever wish. Whatever happens in the rest of this summer, whatever happens the rest of your life, it's important that you are happy, and stay that way. – Aunt Sookie

Summer

Several Months After Summer

I never thought the boy who had taken care of me that summer I lost Aunt Sookie would be the boy who needed taking care of the most, but as I glanced into Nat's sea green eyes and saw the despair in them as he realized what he had done…what I've done…with him, and how Drew had witnessed it, I knew there was more than one Donovan brother to worry about. Only this one was standing in front of me, full body, healthy, and not missing…while the other…

"He's not picking up," Nat said, almost throwing his cell phone against the wall of his college apartment. "Dammit, Drew, pick up your phone…"

"I'm texting him," I say, moving my fingers quickly over my phone.

DREW – I'M SO SORRY. PLEASE CALL ME!

I waited for a minute, hoping he would answer back immediately, like he normally would, but there was nothing.

"Nat, Drew usually texts me right back. He usually answers within seconds…" I could hear my voice rising with worry like the pace of my heartbeat. "Do you think something could've happened to him?" I looked down at the floor. "That's why he's not picking up?" I wanted to believe it was because he was incapacitated, that it wasn't because of what he'd just seen Nat and I doing.

Nat finished buttoning up his shirt and tucking it into his slacks. He had been dressed up for a nice dinner at a restaurant with me after all before I suggested we just go to his apartment near Stanford for dinner. I had wanted to check out his apartment before heading back to Malibu tonight, since it was the first time I've visited him in San Francisco. I had to see where he lived, where he slept, and ate outside of Aunt Sookie's Malibu Pad. Having grown up with him over the years mostly during summers at Aunt Sookie's, I had to get a mental picture of him living, eating, sleeping elsewhere, anywhere besides Aunt Sookie's.

Perhaps, it was me trying to understand why we couldn't be together. Perhaps it was I trying to see that Nat had a life outside of summers in Malibu. That he had a life outside of and without me.

Perfect Summer (Loving Summer #2)

We didn't even get to dinner. As soon as I entered his place, was finally alone with Nat after all the tension we've felt on his private corporate jet that kissing alone couldn't satisfy, through the meeting with his security team at Donovan Dynamics, and on the way to dinner; it all came rushing out. What started out as a kiss became so much more.

It was the first time I've seen him completely naked and had touched him, even tasted all of him. All the working out he'd done during his first semester in college, paid off, and now he was as muscular and chisel as Drew. But had all the steadfastness and maturity of Nat.

He was better than I ever thought he'd be when we got together. His skin against mine, his fingers exploring my body inch by inch. His tongue bringing me to the height of ecstasy. His attentiveness to making me feel pleasure rather than pressure made me feel so at ease with going with the flow that I tried more things with him than I'd ever imagined doing. It was liberating and exhilarating, but so heartfelt. I'd always imagined making love with Nat...what it would be like, ever since I fell hard for him when I was barely thirteen and he was fourteen. I was already in love with him since our first kiss as toddlers. Then when he, Drew, and Rachel came out to the Pad this past summer from San Francisco, after not seeing each other for three summers; I barely recognized how tall, handsome, and hot like a rock star he'd grown into; along with Drew's manwhore transformation and Rachel's rebellious punk Goth look.

Three years made a difference, and suddenly I had intense physical feelings for Nat (and admittedly Drew, who wouldn't if you were female and not a fraternal twin of Drew's like Rachel was). Both of the Donovan brothers were no longer teen boys but young men - having grown taller, broader, muscular and tanned. Both very confident in their own ways, yet still the same boys as I've always known them.

Having such a crush on Nat for so long and finally being able to get together like we did, after all the Christy's and Astor Fairways that came between us, getting physical with him brought me literally to my knees. I just didn't think it would be that good. He was everything I'd dreamed of and more. In the end, being with Nat was an experience I'd always cherish.

Except for the part about hurting Drew.

Drew…what a man. My Drew and the "Drewgasms" he gave me imprinted enough heated memory to last me a lifetime. He had grown into a man, and that first time I saw him stripped down, that time when I nearly had my breakdown, he was there to pick me up, and to make me feel wanted and loved. He was no longer just my best friend Rachel's teasing fraternal twin brother, but one of the hottest guys on the planet.

And he let me have my way with him…which was the biggest mistake I've ever made.

Now I have to pay the price…the price of loving two incredible men, who were brothers, and the price of breaking either or both of their hearts with mine. Whatever mistakes I've made, whatever actions I've taken, there was no turning back. What had been done was done, and now I have to pay the consequences.

Chapter 1

Nat dressed and got ready to go faster than I did, although all I needed to do was slip my dress up further, find my strappy sandals, which had gotten lost somewhere while we were undressing each other, and grab my jacket and purse. I was too worried about Drew to concentrate on what I was doing.

Nat, on the other hand, was cool as ice, helping me dress and then giving me a hand to lead me out of his apartment and into his sleek Aston Martin, where he buckled me in firmly, as though I was a child instead of a woman. With his nice expensive shirt and slacks, his chiseled cheekbones, direct sea green eyes, and luscious full rocker lips, he looked like James Bond or any debonair and confident billionaire's son and future President of

Perfect Summer (Loving Summer #2)

Donovan Dynamics, and I suddenly felt the need to give into Nat's insane natural instincts for control and care. Always having to be the one in control, the independent caretaker of all things and everyone, I wanted to relinquish that burden and let Nat take care of me, for once. Like me, he was good at that. We were so similar in that way, we understood each other.

His dark wavy brown hair with copper highlights mused up on top, fell forward on his forehead as he pulled the straps tight on me, messier than its usual tidy look, giving him a sexy rakish look. "You okay?" he asked, when he looked up.

Even filled with worry for Drew, I couldn't help staring openly at Nat and his almost perfect body. His hands brushing against my thighs while he strapped me into the passenger seat reminded me far too much of his fingers touching my naked thighs and trailing up my legs to my most sensitive core of my body earlier. My body was still aching for his, and I shivered involuntarily.

He saw me looking at him and touched my flushed cheeks gently with his hands. "Don't worry, Summer.

We'll find Drew. I think I know where he is. Despite all of our differences, we're still brothers. I know what he likes and don't like." His eyes burned into mine. "After all, we're both in love with the same girl."

I looked down, unable to meet the intensity in Nat's eyes. Tonight, my crush for Nat had moved beyond a crush. The chemistry between us was undeniable, and the more we clashed, the more we wanted each other. Even now I couldn't help thinking how good he felt against me, how a mere touch from him, the hooding of his eyes, or even the way he would lightly kiss me meant so much more. When I was with him, all logic and sense went flying out my brain.

The only thing that kept me from wanting to unbuckle my seat belt, lean over, and climb onto his lap, was the thought of Drew.

Tonight, although I was hot for Nat as ever, the earth-shattering look on Drew's face when he walked in on Nat pressed against me while we were both half naked, drove home to me how much I cared for Drew, too. I cared for both Donovan brothers more than any boys I've ever known, even subconsciously and then purposely giving up the chance to be with the nicest guy in the universe Astor Fairway, whom any girl would kill to be with. I knew I loved Nat, but I never actually acknowledged loving Drew, too. Now Nat had openly stated it like it was a fact we all knew. He was in love with me. And so was Drew.

"Where do you think he is?" I asked, concentrating on finding Drew. "Do you think…"

"He'll be doing something stupid?" Nat finished my sentence for me. "No. He's smarter than that. He's had a lot of girls before, and he knows how things like this goes."

I turned my face away from Nat, not wanting him to see how much I disliked the idea of Drew with the other girls, and looked out the window at the beautiful night lights that lit up the streets we pass by on our way to where…I don't know. Nat had an idea of where Drew might be. I just wished I did, too.

I checked my phone again to see if he had texted me or left me a message. There was a text I had missed…from Rachel, my best friend and Drew's fraternal twin. Like her twin, Rachel was stunning…with her blue eyes and dark, almost black hair. But unlike Drew, she was slender and small, with blue or sometimes purple chunky streaks in her hair. While Drew was the football star, who won a scholarship to USC and early admissions, Rachel was the Donovan who was into music, films, and acting. She was at Aunt Sookie's Malibu Pad tonight with her boyfriend Ryan, trying to get the most out of the last days of Winter Break…and trying to stay out of her mother's hair.

RACHEL: HEY, HOW'S THE MEETING AT DD?

RACHEL: THOUGHT YOU'LL BE BACK TO THE PAD, BUT IT'S WAY LATE. ARE YOU COMING BACK 2NITE?
JUST SO YOU KNOW, RYAN'S STAYING OVER…

I sighed, and thought about a response. If Drew knew about Ryan staying over at the Pad with Rachel tonight, he'd be banging down the door and chasing Ryan out. Ryan staying over was codename for Rachel having sex with Ryan at the Pad, which Drew shouldn't have any problems with, considering how he'd have so many one-night stands with the girls from school, from everywhere, even once at Disneyland when I was out on my first date with Astor that he was known to have a Drew Effect on them.

I was about to text back to Rachel about what Drew would say, but decided against it. Rachel was eighteen, like Drew. Like me. We were legally adults now. Nat was nineteen. In a way, although I wanted to tell Rachel to be careful of rushing into things too fast, I refrained from saying anything like that. She was an adult now and old enough to make her own decisions…yet…

I texted her back.

ME: I DON'T THINK I'LL MAKE IT BACK TONIGHT. CALL DREW. I CAN'T FIND HIM. WORRIED.

The instant I hit "send", there was a text.

RACHEL: HOLY CRAP. WHAT HAPPENED?

WHY IS DREW MISSING?

ME: DON'T FREAK, BUT DREW WALKED IN ON NAT AND I.

RACHEL: HOLY MAJOR CRAP. THAT EXPLAINS WHY.

ME: I THINK HE'S ANGRY AND HURT. HE WON'T ANSWER MY CALLS. NOR NAT'S.

RACHEL: I JUST TEXTED HIM. I'LL TRY CALLING HIM.

ME: TEXT ME AS SOON AS YOU HEAR FROM HIM.

RACHEL: I WILL. GOTTA GO.

ME: BYE

RACHEL: SAYONA

I glanced at Nat whose eyes were concentrated on the road, his hands gripped tight around the wheel like some kind of death trap. His jaws were clenched, and the muscles around his neck were bulging. He looked more worried than I've ever seen him. But there was something else there, behind his eyes…another emotion I haven't seen on his face for a long time…fear.

"Nat," I asked softly. "Are you alright?"

For a brief second Nat's shoulders tensed, as though I had startled him out of his thoughts, and then it relaxed. He visibly took a breath before turning to face me, his face suddenly calm and collected. "I'm fine," he said. "Just concentrating on the road. It can be treacherous winding through these hills."

I looked out the window, and saw how the car was making its way up hill. It was a steep climb with turns that were sudden and sharp. I could see how Nat needed to concentrate so all I said was, "good."

After some time, we did make it to the top, and from there, we drove a few blocks until we came up to a driveway fortressed by a gilded wrought iron gate. Nat pressed a button on his console, and the gate swung open, allowing us to drive into the large courtyard and into one of the garages.

When Nat parked the Aston, he came over to help

me out, taking my hand in his and walking me over to the entrance. "Nat," I gushed. "your home…it's lovely. I knew your parents' company were doing so well, but I didn't think…your home is as big as a castle."

Nat laughed. "No, not that big, Summer, but I personally think it's way over the top. I mean, we don't need to have turrets. But thank you. I shouldn't be complaining. It is a nice house, and Mom designed it. It's what makes her feel safe and secure."

"I think it looks majestic," I said. "Like a modern castle out of a fairy tale. If it makes your mother happy, then that's what counts. I love it!" I said.

Nat smiled slowly, making my heart melt at the boyish grin he had, which brought out his dimples. "It's not the Pad, though, Summer. It's a million years away from the Pad."

I came up to Nat, took his hand in mine, and leaned in to look him square in his eyes. "No, it isn't, but that's alright. It doesn't have to be. I love Aunt Sookie's house, but that's hers, and it has a very special place in my heart, and yours, but this place…this beautiful castle your family built – your mom, dad, Drew, and Rachel; this place is special too. It's your own. It's the Donovans' place. Your den away from the lions."

"How appropriate," Nat said. "It is like a den. The Donovan Den. When my parents built this monstrosity of a house, it was so different from the carefree beach house we were so used to. It felt like a fortress, Summer, with the gates, the turrets, the thick walls and high hedges. Come on…let's go inside. I'll give you a tour. You'll see."

He took my hand and led me inside the house from an entranceway in the garage. As soon as I stepped into the house, I felt at ease. The house was more modern than I expected, but still had the elegance of a French country estate manor. A warm light softly lit the hallway we were in, and Nat continued holding my hand as we walked into the marble foyer, pass a massive double staircase, and into the living room.

"Hungry?" he asked. "You must be…we skipped dinner hours ago."

"And went straight to dessert," I muttered softly,

blushing, my lips slightly parted as I licked them without thinking.

Nat moved up close to me, pressing me against the wall and kissed me, his mouth hot and passionate against mine. "I like having dessert first," he whispered into my ears. He kissed my bottom lip, moving it into his mouth to suck on. The intensity of it between his lips made me moan. "I know we're supposed to get something to eat and to show you around, but all I can think about right now, Summer, is devouring you."

I kissed him back, "who needs food when we have other needs to fulfill."

"Exactly," Nat said, pressing into me so I can feel how much he wanted me. He kissed my ear and gently bit on it, whispering, "Summer, why can't I stop wanting you? I have so much on my mind, so much I have to do at the moment; but all I can think about is wanting you." He kissed me hard on my mouth and brushed his tongue against mine, causing me to arch my back and press my breasts forward into his chest. "I'm going to give you the quick version of a tour, Summer. Hang on tight."

He hitched me up with his hands so my legs were wrapped around his waist. When I leaned my head close to his, his lips inched up to capture mine before he started walking with me hanging onto him like a Siamese twin. He walked quickly through a large French country kitchen with double stainless steel refrigerators, a professional grade stove, and everything that made it a chef's dream kitchen barely muttering, "Kitchen" before increasing his pace until we were going up the stairs and into a hallway full of doors. "Guest rooms, theater room, game room, a sauna, the gym room..." he continued announcing while continuing on with the tour, with me riding against him, every brush against him sending a pleasurable sensation through me. "And finally," we stepped into a room that I recognized immediately as Nat's room. Clean sleek lines, no nonsense, tidy, but still friendly and grounded. Also masculine with a massive dark oak bed in the center of the room lined with grey and white linen. In the corner of his room was a guitar next to a woodsy dresser drawer with some photo frames on it. Pictures of Nat with Drew and

Rachel. Pictures of the whole family. Then a photo of me with him when we were thirteen, the year they moved.

Nat threw me down on his bed, and collapsed next to me, breathing hard. "Just need to catch my breath for a sec. But that was harder than it looked," he said between breaths.

I grinned. "So you are human after all." I touched his chest, feeling him breathe hard in and out. "I always thought you were made of steel, you know," I said.

"Superman?" Nat arched his eyebrows.

"No, the Tin Man," I answered back. I settled my head against his chest, turning my ear to listen to his heartbeat. "I sometimes wondered if you had a heart."

Nat winced. "Summer. I'm sorry for ignoring you those years after we moved. I'm so sorry I hurt you in any way." He pulled me closer to his chest and kissed the top of my head as he held me tight. "Although we've had hundreds of miles separating us, although I've kept my distance...I want you to know, Summer, that I had always loved you. Then and now."

Perfect Summer (Loving Summer #2)

My heart was beating like a drum as his words sunk into my brain. Nat had always loved me, as I loved him. He had always felt the same way…only why didn't he show it? Tears of frustration began forming in my eyes. "All those years, Nat, why didn't you tell me?" I cried. "I thought you didn't care for me, that my love for you was just a hopeless dream. Why couldn't you tell me how you felt instead of ignoring for years?"

Nat's face was torn. There was love in his eyes, as well as despair. "Because Summer, I didn't want to hurt you." He got up and went to the photo of us on his bureau, picking it up. "That summer we moved was one of the hardest ones for me. I knew then that I had fallen in love with you, and that we couldn't be together. I thought if I stayed away, I could get over loving you, but…it didn't. It made this feeling I have for you more solid, more real. It wasn't just a short crush, but the real thing."

"But not telling me how you felt, hurt even more," I said. "I thought it was because I wasn't pretty enough. That I was too fat or not popular enough. I went through some major self-esteem lows, thinking it was all my fault, it was all because of something I did or couldn't live up to." I gulped, as I choke back some tears. "I hated myself for years because I didn't think I was good enough for you, Nat. That you left me in Malibu, was happy to move away from me, because I wasn't what you wanted."

"That's so not true, Summer," Nat said gently, his voice choked up as much as mine. "It was the exact opposite." He raised his fingers and brushed away my tears. "Why do you think I called this place a fortress? Why did you think I was so unhappy being in this grand dream house my parents built?" He leaned in and kissed away the remaining tears on my cheeks and my eyelids. "I was miserable being here. I hated being away from you, hated being away from the beach and Malibu. That was home to me, Summer. Wherever you are, will be home to me." He flipped me over on my back then, with a passion that knocked the breath out of me, and crushed his lips on mine.

I kissed him back hard, entwining my fingers into his hair as I brought him closer to me. We kissed and kissed until we were both breathless. When Nat finally pulled back to look me in the eyes, he said, "I love you, Summer, and I want you. Don't. You. Ever. Doubt. That."

Chapter 2

I continued staring at Nat's handsome face when my phone went off.

"Hey, it's Rachel," she said. "I just heard back from Drew!"

"You did?" I nearly shouted with relief. "How is he?"

Nat sat up in bed and pulled me up. His phone had started ringing at the same time.

"He's fine," Rachel said. "He just texted me. I actually didn't talk to him in person, but he said he was fine."

"Where is he? Why did he contact you instead of Nat or me? We've been trying to get in touch with him for hours…"

"I texted him saying I'm staying in Malibu tonight. Not to worry, since I'll be with Ryan all alone at the Malibu Pad since you're not going to be there tonight," Rachel said. "Guessed that got his attention. You know, overprotective twin brother and all."

"Is he there?" I asked, noticing Nat getting out of bed to pick up his phone. "Did he take the private jet over?" I watched Nat walked over to his desk, pulled out a pad of paper, searched for a pen, found one, and then began jotting down something, while speaking on his phone.

"No," Rachel said. "He's in San Fran, but he did send me a text saying he'll kick my butt and Ryan's butt if he finds Ryan at the Pad tomorrow. Like he's one to talk."

"He's going to Malibu?" I asked. "Why?"

"Beats me, but I thought he was planning on moving out here to start at USC this semester," Rachel said. "Wasn't that his plans?"

"Yes," I said, remembering how excited Drew was about getting his football scholarship to USC along with his early admissions to start this semester. "So he's moving into the Pad tomorrow?" I asked.

"You invited his sorry ass to?" Rachel asked. "Pardon my French, but after all the worry he put all of us through tonight..."

"I'm just glad he's safe," I said. "And I did say when he moved down to LA for USC, he can stay here with me for school."

"Uh huh," Rachel said. I can hear the question in her voice.

"As friends, Rachel," I said. "Aunt Sookie's place is as much part of his, Nat's, and yours as it is mine." I gave a sigh of relief. "You're all welcome to stay, you know that."

"Sure," Rachel said. "I do. But is it wise?"

"What do you mean by that?" I asked.

"Nothing," Rachel said. "I just know that there's something between you, Nat, and Drew right now, and well..."

"I know," I said. "I can't talk about it right now. By the way, Nat's here." I walked over to Nat where he was just ending his call. He had a worried look on his face, which made me want to kiss and make better. "Hey, is everything alright?"

"Just heard from the security team at Donovan Dynamics."

"Oh," I said. I didn't think Nat would've contacted them to find Drew.

"Someone spotted Drew. He was driving down Highway 101, heading towards Malibu. He was about a third of the way there."

"Maybe we can catch up to him," I suggested. "We're headed back anyways."

Nat nodded. "We can at least take the jet back, but there is no way we can stop where Drew is. We'll head back to Malibu."

"Okay," I said, "At least we know where he's heading so we can meet him. Hey Rachel," I said into my phone. "Did you hear any of that?"

"What? Um…I was busy," Rachel said. "Stop that," she said.

"Stop what?" I said.

"Oh nothing," Rachel said. Then she giggled. "Ryan!"

"Look Rachel," I said. "Looks like Drew's heading to Malibu. Nat and I will be going there, too."

"Great, seems like everyone's heading back, Ryan," Rachel said away from the phone. "We can't have our marathon sex session tonight."

"Rachel," I said. "I can hear you."

"Good," she said. "Maybe you should have one too with either Nat or Drew and get it over with. Then maybe this whole tension between you three will go away."

"I'm not even going to answer that, Rachel," I said. "See you soon."

"Okay," Rachel said. "See you soon!"

I ended the call and walked over to Nat. He was looking down, at his desk, his hands gripped tight on the paper he used to jot down some information. "Hey," I said, slipping my arms through his to circle his waist from behind while resting my chin on his shoulders. "We found him." I smiled. "I was so worried, Nat."

"I know," Nat said, turning around to face me. "Me, too." He slipped the piece of paper he had in his hand into his pants pocket before cupping my face with it, and tracing his thumb over my lips, making me tingle all over. "As much as I want him away from you, Summer, so I can have you all to myself, he's still my annoying brother. I have to watch out for him, too." He dropped his hand from my face then. "Come on, it's time I took you back home."

**

We were heading down the stairs to the foyer when the front door opened, and a familiar deep female voice sang up to us. I haven't heard the voice in years, but I could recognize the husky richness of it anywhere. It belonged to Nadine Donovan, the Donovan brothers and Rachel's mother.

"Nat, baby, are you home?" she called up. I saw your car parked in the garage just now. Where are you baby?"

She rounded the corner just as Nat and I reached the bottom of the stairs to stand close to each other in the foyer.

"Ah, there you are!" she said, her blue eyes twinkling with happiness at seeing her eldest son return home from college. She went right up to him and hugged him tightly. "I hoped you aced your finals," she said. "Okay, not hoped, I know you would." She pulled back to look at him. "How was it? Your first finals of the semester?"

Nat grinned. "I did pretty well, Mom."

"Of course you would, Nat," Nadine said. "You never disappoint…my perfect son, unlike your father."

"Mom," Nat said, "we have guest." He winked at me while Nadine glanced over at me.

Nadine's big blue eyes took me all in and looked confused at first. Then her eyes lit up in recognition. "Summer?"

"Mrs. Donovan," I smiled at her. She hadn't aged a bit since I last saw her three years ago. With her long dark hair, blue eyes, and flawless skin, she looked very much like Drew and Rachel's mother. Stunning and beautiful, like they were. "You look fabulous," I said, walking up to her and giving her a hug.

"My goodness, Summer Jones, you are a beauty!" Nadine exclaimed. "Sookie wasn't kidding when she said you've grown into the kind of woman men lose their minds over." She stared at me for a moment and there was a touch of wistful sadness in her voice, "you remind me so much of Sookie when she was younger. That vivaciousness and poise."

"Thank you," I said. "She was quite a woman, and I'm proud to be compared to her, Mrs. Donovan."

"Please, Nadine…" she said. "We've known each other for how long? We're family, and one day, I hope you will be officially a Donovan."

I turned crimson as I glanced over at Nat then.

He was looking at me, his sea green eyes burning into me with an intense desire. Did Mrs. Donovan know something I didn't know?

"It's still too early to say," I said, barely looking at Nat, while focusing my attention on Nadine. "I'm young, and there are so many things I'd like to do before…"

Nadine smile and waved her hand. "Of course you're still young, Summer. You want to experience the world, see places, meet lots of people, and find yourself before you become a Donovan, but…" she looked over at Nat. "If the right person comes along into your life, don't waste the opportunity." She sighed. "I kept telling Sookie that when we were in college, and she half-listened to me. Turned down the right guy for her, and ended up marrying someone whom all she got was that beach house."

"Mom," Nat said suddenly. "Summer and I have to get going. I'll be back tomorrow to take you to see the new doctor." He leaned in and kissed Nadine on the forehead.

"Alright," Nadine said. She turned to me and pulled me to her for a hug. "I'm so glad to see you again. I heard so much about you from Sookie and the kids. They all adore you. Come back out and stay anytime."

Still stunned by what Nadine said about Sookie marrying the wrong guy, and giving up the right one; I stood there with my mouth open until Nat leaned in and whispered. "Come on Summer. We've got to go."

"Thank you, Nadine," I said going off with Nat to the car. "Someday, I'd like to hear all about Aunt Sookie when she was my age even about Aunt Sookie at any age. I wished I had the chance to know more about her when she was younger, before she became Aunt Sookie. Well, take good care of yourself."

Nadine smiled wistfully. "I will, Sookie," she said. "Anytime."

Sookie?

I looked over at Nat just when he hurried me to the car. I heard a bit about Nadine's mental state, how she suffered from bouts of depression, but I didn't think she was becoming delusional, as well.

Nat didn't say anything about the slip, but kept his eyes on the road, driving as fast as he could. Maybe he didn't hear it? Or maybe he was so used to it, it didn't surprise him. For me, it made me love him more for being so courageous and brave living with and dealing with his mother's condition. It couldn't be easy watching your own parents or someone you love dearly, slowly lose their minds.

Chapter 3

We got to the Malibu Pad in record time, and waited with Rachel and Ryan for Drew to show up. We waited for hours, and finally went off to sleep. Nat in the room he shared with Drew, and Rachel and Ryan in the spare guest room. No doubt, trying to commence their interrupted sex marathon.

I was sound asleep in my own bed when I heard the door creak open and footsteps entering. I thought it was Rachel at first, but felt someone slip in besides me in bed. Someone with a large hard-on pressed against my back. I was going to turn around when I felt hands slip underneath my t-shirt and reach up to cup my breasts, before his fingers circled and teased my nipples to hard perfection.

It was too dark to see anything, but his hands felt familiar, and I leaned into his chest with a soft moan, closing my eyes. I liked this sneaky, playful side of Nat. I smiled, enjoying his hands' onslaught on my breasts and skin. I turned towards him and felt a cool wetness on my breasts, as his tongue continued what his fingers started, making me squirm with mounting pleasure.

While his mouth devoured every inch of my breasts and made its way to my shoulders, neck, and now lips, I reached down to touch his bare butt, pulling him closer to me. He was completely naked on top of me, and my hands found its way across smooth rippled abs, chiseled chest, and a trimmed waistline.

"You are so tempting," I said. "I normally wouldn't let a guy into my bed like this, but…"

His mouth silenced mine as his tongue met mine, shooting a lightning bolt of pleasure through me. I arched my back and moaned, wanting to get closer to him that I wrapped my legs around his waist, and dug my feet into his back, pushing his hard-on to press up against the thin fabric of my panties, barely covering the part of me that was burning for him. He let out a groan this time, and I took the moment to start kissing his chest and trailed down his skin.

I had made my way to his chest and began licking him when his hands reach down and ripped my panties off. Expecting him to finally enter me, I pulled back. Instead, his fingers found me below.

Which he used to torment me to the point of ecstasy as wave after wave of pleasure crested through me.

My moan was captured by his mouth covering mine, kissing me as my entire body shattered with the most intense pleasure I've ever experienced.

When I subsided, he kissed me hard and pulled me into his arms, crushing me with strong arms, making me feel protected and revered. I kissed him back, matching his fervor kiss by kiss until he was groaning. He finally pulled back, panting for breath, as I gasped for air. "I love you so much, Summer," he said. "I've been in love with you for as long as I can remember." Then he groaned with pain and frustration. "I want to be everything for you. To be your first, to be the love of your life...but I can't. It took me this long to realize I never would. I never could. He would always be first. Even with you. But now you know, Summer. You know what it's like with me. How I can rock your world. How special it is with us. So, every time you're with him, know that you're not with me. That you…" his fingers stroked my sensitive skin, making me burn with desire for him, "will not be feeling this with me, feeling this good." He plunged his fingers deep into me and I let out a moan. "That this, dear Summer, will be the last time you get to feel this…" he worked me over and over again until I was climaxing.

When I subsided, he kissed me hard as though he was trying to get as much into it, commit it to memory. "I want this, too, Summer, but I want more. But, you can't give me that. So from now on, Summer, I'll leave you alone, leave you be." He abruptly got out of bed, and kissed me one last time. "With Nat."

Nat? My eyes shot open searching the dark room. But he was gone. My phantom lover was gone as quickly and mysteriously as he entered it. Whoever he was, he wasn't Nat. I got up and pulled on a robe before shuffling out to the living room and to the front door, just barely seeing the headlights of a sports car pull out of the driveway and into the night. I tried to remember where I've seen that car before but couldn't. It was one I've never seen before.

I was closing the door when strong arms wrapped around me from behind, followed by a kiss on my collarbone and shoulders. "Why are you up so early, Summer?" Nat's husky voice asked. "Can't sleep?"

"No," I answered simply. "Heard something..." I turned around and looked into Nat's eyes. "I think Drew was just here, but he left."

It was too dark to see Nat's expression at that moment, but I can feel his shoulder muscles tense at the mention of Drew's name. He didn't say anything then, but led me to the sofa where I sank into his chest and arms, burying my head against him. His arms wrapped around me protectively yet gently, and I felt myself relaxing. The entire day had exhausted me, along with the tryst I've had. I tried to stay up, knowing how Nat probably wanted to ask more about Drew's visit, but couldn't keep my eyes open. The last thing I saw before sleep overcame me was Nat's loving eyes looking down at my face, and his fingertips tracing my cheeks and lips. I was out before I can see the worry flicker across his eyes or hear him whisper, "I love you so much, Summer, and I won't let anyone hurt you...even Drew."

Chapter 4

I couldn't stop thinking about my phantom lover the next day. I was almost certain it was Drew, not Nat. I tried texting Drew again, but he didn't answer.

It was so unusual of him not to, and because of what happened last night, I wanted more than ever to reach him, to find out what happened, to talk to him.

I knew he hadn't been in touch with Nat because Nat was back on the phone with his security team early this morning, asking about the whereabouts of Drew. Turned out, he did make it down into town briefly, but they lost him when he drove farther south from Malibu, heading into Los Angeles.

"Don't worry, Summer," Nat said at breakfast this morning. "We'll find him. The good news is, that he seems to be fine if he could drive that much. He's not driving recklessly, too, so his head seems clear enough."

"Nat…" I began, not knowing how to tell him that I was with Drew last night, or at least I thought I was, unless I dreamt it. If so, then Drew was perfectly fine and in control of himself. *And of every part of me…* I blushed remembering how he was able to get me to have multiple orgasms just last night.

"What, Summer?" Nat put down his fork on his plate to give me his full attention. "What is it?"

I began, but stopped myself. What if I had dreamt it all…was so worried about Drew and was secretly lusting after him so much that my mind imagined all of that? I was the only one who saw the car take off from the driveway. Even Nat's security team said Drew drove further south of Malibu. He probably didn't stop.

Nat's eyes rove over my face with the most adoring look. It was the look I've always wanted to see him shower me with…that look of utter love and adoration, the look of a man in love with a woman. He took my hand in his and squeezed it. "Whatever it is, Summer, you can tell me. I want open communication between us. I don't ever want you to have any doubts about us or how I feel about you."

I smiled and squeezed his hand back.

"Talking about open communication," Nat looked uncomfortable. "I hate to leave you so soon, but I have to go back to San Fran. I told Mom I'll take her to see a new specialist with her."

"She seems happy and fine last night," I said, *except for her calling me Sookie.* "Bubbly even. I can see how she and Aunt Sookie could have been best friends for so long."

"Yeah, Mom was always liked that in the beginning. Lively and vivacious. Positive and upbeat. She was Dad's backbone, his motivator. Then one day, she had a complete personality change, like having the light and life sucked out of her." Nat looked disgusted. "Now, she has to rely on medication to keep her from slipping into that darkness. Mom isn't Mom anymore without those pills."

I reached over to touch his face. "Nat, if you want me to go with you back to San Fran today, I can. You're not alone in caring for your mom. I'm here, too."

Nat smiled and leaned over to give me a lingering soft kiss. "I know." Then he got up and walked over to his leather overnight bag, grabbed it, and came over. "Summer," he said, crushing me against him. "I promise to call you everyday but one kiss isn't going to be enough to tide me over for a week before I can come down here to be with you." With that, he pushed me to the wall, dropped his bag, and entwined his fingers into mine, pushing my hands up against the wall while he kissed me soundly and deeply before he left for the hangar to go back to San Francisco and the Donovan's Den.

I was returning back to the kitchen to start the wash when the door to the spare guest room opened, and Rachel came out wearing an oversized black punk rock t-shirt, obviously Ryan's. Ryan followed right behind Rachel, wearing only his boxers and no shirt. He was good-looking in a pale and thin Goth way that suited Rachel, but I averted my eyes. It was strange seeing Rachel as this sexual being, having known her since she and I were only four or five years old.

Perfect Summer (Loving Summer #2)

"Good morning!" Rachel practically sang.

"Looks like you've had a great night," I said, preparing her breakfast for her at the counter. Nat had left a skillet full of eggs with roasted red pepper, turkey sausages, and potatoes he made this morning for everyone. I scooped a good size portion onto white plates and took it over to Rachel and taking the seat next to her.

Rachel beamed back at me. "Ryan really knows how to push my buttons." She leaned over. "So...how was Nat and you? I know. I hate to think you can be with one of my brothers, but...the way Nat and you couldn't take your hands off each other last night when you got in...I assumed, you two would hook up, after all these years. Summer, after all these years, Nat's finally returned your feelings. I am so happy for you because I know Nat will treat you right. He's such a gentleman and a good brother. If he wasn't my brother, and if I wasn't so into Ryan, I would pick Nat."

"I thought you were Team Astor," I said.

"I was, but now that you're not even remotely going there with him, unless you surprise us somehow, then I would think you are genuinely and utterly torn between my two hot brothers."

"Um…" I began. "We did get physical, but there are still some obstacles."

"Not as big as the ones you and Astor had, though, Summer." Rachel made a sad face. "Okay, I was secretly hoping you and Astor would last. He's such a nice guy, and so good-looking. Not to mention, fun to be around. You know when he heard you mention that I wanted to give acting a shot, he immediately set me up to meet with his agent and manager. Next month when I can fly back down here."

I smiled, thinking about Astor. He was incredible, and so perfect. It was hard to believe a guy like him could exist.

"He did asked about you when I saw him at the school yesterday," Rachel said. "He helped me teach one of the classes, and well, we all had a great time…one of the better classes I've taught."

"So he's no longer this intimidating star you see onscreen?" I asked.

"No, I'm way past that now. Now, he's just Astor, a super nice guy with good looks and natural charm. He kinda have that sexy dangerousness to him, too, if you see his films. Reminds me of that actor, Alex Pettyfer."

"Careful Rachel," I said, "don't let Ryan hear how much you're gushing about Astor, he might think you'll dump him for golden boy."

Rachel blushed. "I wouldn't! Ryan is incredible, too. In his own way. Plus, Astor only has eyes for you. He kept asking about you, how you were doing, and when will you start at USC." Rachel stopped. "He's staying in town for a while before going off to film his new project, which, he said, would be filmed in Vegas for a few weeks."

"That's great, Rachel. I'm happy for him, but he and I are no longer together. We broke up, remember. First me with him, and then he publicly with me. You had something to do with it, remember?"

Rachel shrugged. "Yeah, but you're still friends. He's still part of our lives, as long as we're all tied to Aunt

Sookie's Acting Academy. Astor said he wanted to talk to you, Summer…about the Academy. He had some really good ideas for the school."

"Great," I said. "I'm heading over to the Academy this morning. Maybe I'll see him there."

"As a matter of fact…" Rachel grinned slyly. "He's teaching my class this morning for me so I can spend the day with Ryan. I head back to San Fran tomorrow, Summer, to start the last semester of school. It sucks. I'm the only one who isn't in college yet. Even Drew got early admissions."

I went over to hug Rachel. "It'll go by fast, and then you'll be regretting not enjoying your last semester in high school. I know I did. I can't believe I start at USC this week." I went over to the door, grabbed my purse and keys, and said, "I have to run. This is probably the only day I can spend at the Academy working on the budget and schedules before starting college. I'll be there all day, if you need to find me."

"Okay, good," Rachel said, munching on her breakfast. "Ryan had something planned for me today so I don't know where I'd be, but call me or text me if you need me. And if I hear anything from Drew, I'll let you know."

"Great!" I gave her a thumbs up, and ran to the large SUV I inherited from Aunt Sookie, got in, and made my way through the side streets to the old converted theater now acting school Aunt Sookie ran for nearly a decade.

Everything looked clean and tidy when I stepped into the theater. Rachel surprised me with how well she ran the place when I was gone for the day. I went down the aisles and headed to the back where Aunt Sookie's office was. Now that Winter's break was over, I had to begin planning for the Summer classes, especially Summer Camp for the kids. It was the busiest time for the Academy, and I couldn't miss getting ready for the season. As I made my way over to the office, I noticed there was a light coming from underneath the door. So, it seemed Rachel had forgotten to turn off all the lights and lock up last night.

Too much Ryan on the brain, I thought.

How lucky Rachel was to be able to enjoy such an uncomplicated relationship with Ryan, although, if Ryan wasn't in the picture...I wondered if she would make her moves on Astor.

When I thought about my ex, I only have fond memories of him. Astor did sweep me off my feet enough for me to forget about my long-time crush on Nat, and even distract me from the insanely sexy vibes I kept getting from being anywhere near Drew.

Speaking of Drew...I checked my messages for any missed calls and texts on my phone. I was still worried about Drew, but less than before I found out he was heading down to Southern Cal. When he contacted Rachel instead of me nor Nat, I got it. He was angry at us. And he wanted to avoid us.

But he was Drew, and no matter how much Drew could get under my skin, could screw things up, or could make me get so frustrated at him; he was still Drew.

I texted him:

ME: DREW, I'M SORRY. I NEVER MEANT TO HURT YOU. I STILL CARE ABOUT YOU AND AM WORRIED ABOUT YOU. YOU SAID YOU WOULD BE HERE FOR ME. THAT YOU WOULD ALWAYS BE THERE FOR ME. WELL, I NEED YOU. AND I NEED TO KNOW YOU'RE ALRIGHT. IF YOU'RE AROUND TODAY, I'LL BE AT THE ACADEMY ALL DAY. HOPE TO SEE YOU SOON. I LOVE YOU.

I sighed, feeling the exact places that was heated up last night from my phantom lover, and shook my head to clear those thoughts. If my phantom lover was Drew, he sure knew how to exact revenge on me, getting me aroused and heated like that, only to leave me and tell me I won't ever experience that again with him.

Fine. If Drew was angry at me, and didn't want any contact with me, then I'll leave him alone. He knew how he could reach me. I wasn't going to spend another moment longer worrying about him when I had other things on my mind…like trying to make ends meet with running Aunt Sookie's Academy.

Kailin Gow

I reached out to open the handle on the office door, when it flew open, and a large body crashed into me, sending my phone flying across the room, while knocking me on the ground, sprawled down.

My summer beach dress flew up around me, and before I can push my skirt down, a body landed on top of me, pushing me down hard enough to hit my right elbow against the concrete floor. Intense pain shot through my elbow that brought tears to my eyes. I screamed out, and tried to kick the person off of me, but grubby hands covered my mouth, while another hand fumbled with my panties, groping.

I was pinned by my arms and legs, and the person was too close to me where I couldn't get a good look at him. When he moved his face close enough where I could smell the rancid cigarette breath, I did what I learned to do in self-defense class. I head butted him as hard as I could, causing him to jump off of me.

"Bitch!" an unfamiliar voice grunted.

Perfect Summer (Loving Summer #2)

I tried to get up, but my right arm felt numb. Useless. I couldn't even use it to help me stand. But my mouth was free from his foul dirty hands, and I yelled, "Help! Anyone! Help!"

I didn't know if there was anyone else in the theater. The first class would be beginning in fifteen minutes, and I thought I had unlocked the front doors to let students in early. I hoped and pray a student would arrive early enough...

In the dark of the theater, I saw the man get up, and was heading back towards me when a second figure walked in through the side door of the theater and rushed him, crushing him against the wall of the theater.

The man was stunned for a minute, but got up and ran out the door.

I tried to get up again, but fell back down. My right arm was numb, and a sharp pain ran through my back. I could only stare straight up, feeling like a useless rag doll.

"Summer?" the newcomer said, coming toward me.

My breath caught in my throat as I realized who it was.

"Summer," there was such pain and concern in his beautiful masculine voice. "My gosh, I wished I'd gotten here sooner so that son of a bitch couldn't hurt you like this."

"Drew," I croaked out, trying to hold back my tears. "You got my message. You're here."

Drew looked at me, his face worried, but full of pain, anger, and love. "I can't stay away from you, even if I tried. And I did, believe me, I did."

"You got here just in time," I said. "I don't know what would've happened if you didn't." A shudder ran through me then, and Drew noticed.

He gently bent down, touching my face. "Hush, Summer. Don't even think about it. I'm here, and if I let myself think of what could've happen to you if I came a second too late, I'd rush out there, find the guy, and beat him to an inch of his life." He bent down to try lifting me so I can get on my feet, but I winced with pain when he touched my arm.

"Can you walk?" Drew asked. He gently touched my arm. "Your arm…"

"I think it's broken," I said. "I'm just hoping I don't lose my volleyball scholarship to USC now," I said, biting my lips. "What a way to start college in a couple of days."

"It'll heal," Drew said. "We get sports injuries all the time, but they heal." His eyes took in the remainder of me, lying prone on the hard floor. When his eyes lingered longer over my breasts and my barely-clad lower half; I couldn't help think of the phantom from last night.

In the distance, I heard several voices.

"Oh, crap, class is starting in a few minutes," I said, trying to get up again.

"I need to get you to the doctor's," Drew said. "To get you checked out. You'll have to cancel the class."

"I can't do that," I said. "Maybe if I can sit, I can direct them what to do today."

"If you're up to it," Drew said.

"Can you help me up?" I asked.

"You don't have to ask," Drew said, placing his strong arms underneath me and lifting me up to carry me into the main classroom.

He made me feel tiny in his arms, and I was grateful having him there with me. "I would never have guessed this would happen to me," I joked. "That I would have your strong arms around me, carrying me around like I weighed nothing."

"You do!" Drew smiled then, adjusting me so I was more comfortable. My hair slipped forward and brush across his face. His smile disappeared. For a second his face froze, and his eyes grew serious as he stared down at me, darting between my eyes and mouth. From beneath his t-shirt, I could feel his heart quicken as his grip on my waist tightened. "Gosh, Summer," he said softly. "You smell," he swallowed. "Good enough to eat."

It became hard to breathe, as my breath quickened to match his. I didn't dream about Drew showing up in my bedroom last night, did I? I had to find out.

Perfect Summer (Loving Summer #2)

"Drew…about last night…did you come by the Pad? Were you in Malibu?"

Drew's eyes met mine, and it was dark with desire. "What about last night?" he asked.

I looked away. It had to be Drew last night. Who else could it have been?

"Look, Summer," Drew said as we got closer to the back of the stage where we could enter to go onstage. "What went down at Nat's apartment, I'm trying to deal with that right now."

"I'm sorry you saw us together," I said. "But technically, you and I aren't together, either."

"I know," Drew said fiercely. "But I wanted to change that. You know I do."

"I thought you just wanted the physical with me, Drew, like you do with all the girls."

Drew's head fell back as though his face was slapped. "That's all you think I think of you?"

"I know that's what you want with me, Drew," I said.

"I do," Drew admitted, his eyes devouring my body appreciatively. "But with you...I want so much more, Summer. So much more than you're willing to give me." He paused, "Every single touch, every single look you give me, I cherish."

"Drew," I began. "I'm sorry..."

"I know, Summer. I know you can't help wanting Nat. It's the same old story. Nothing's changed over the years. Seeing you and Nat together just confirmed it. I have to protect myself, Summer, from getting my heart broken each time I see you with Nat. Or anyone other than me."

"What are you saying, Drew?" I asked.

"I'm saying that I'm through trying to win you, Summer. I have to move on, stop wishing things were different between us, and finding that someone who can appreciate me for who I am, not what I could be."

"I always did appreciate you for who you are now, Drew..."

"I know, Summer, and it's one of the many things I love about you. But like I said, I can't stay around waiting forever, and I certainly can't stand seeing you and Nat together ever again, without wanting to rip off his head and claiming you on the spot like a caveman marking his woman."

"So until you realize who you really want to be with, Summer, all I am going to be is a friend. Nothing else. Not even with benefits. Is that clear?"

I nodded, not liking what I was hearing, but unable to give him what he wanted.

"Good," he said, walking on stage with me in his arms to face an entire class of acting students. "I'm glad that's clear, because if we were more than friends, I'd be out of my mind jealous and suspicious with what I'm seeing right now."

Drew set me down in a folding chair right when a tall, muscular, and strikingly handsome blonde young man walked over to us, a look of concern clouding his perfect features.

"Summer!" Astor exclaimed. "Summer," he lifted me from the chair to put his arms around me, crushing me to his chest. "I missed you so much, I couldn't wait to come back into town."

"Ouch," I winced, feeling my arm hang limply at my side.

Astor stepped back. "Hey, I'm sorry. Your arm...you've hurt it." He looked over at Drew. "What happened?"

Drew stared stonily at Astor, as though he couldn't stand the sight of him. Astor ignored him and looked back at me. "You need to get that looked at, Summer."

"Astor," I said, truly happy to see him again. He had a way with him that always made me feel beautiful and special. "It's good to see you, but I can't right now. I have to work on the budget and the summer class set ups today. If I don't, then it won't be ready in time for summer. I'll have missed the window to advertise for it."

Astor's grin was gone, and he placed both hands on my shoulders. "No, Summer. Taking care of yourself is more important than all of this."

"But…" I began. "When I start college, I know I'm going to be buried with school work, and catching up with the semester. It won't be easy…but I think I can handle it, as long as I'm organized about it."

"Did Rachel tell you I wanted to talk to you about the Academy?" Astor asked.

I nodded, looking into his eyes, trying to read into it, but couldn't. "I'll explain later what I have in mind, but in the meantime, you have a class waiting to learn all about characterization. Mind if I teach it today? It's something I wanted to hone up on too so teaching it will only help me re-learn it."

"No, I don't mind," I said, easily charmed out of my pants by Astor.

"Good because I want you to concentrate on taking care of you. I'd tell Drew to take you to the doctor's, but from that look on his face, if I even look his way, we'd be in fist fight. What happened to you, and why is he here?"

"Well, I was attacked just now in the office."

Astor's face filled with concern and then anger. "Who was it?"

"I don't know, it was dark, and I couldn't see his face."

"Do you think it's a stalker?" Astor crossed his arms. "The same people who broke your windshield and tried to burn down the school?"

"Could be related," I said. "I don't know. I don't even know how he could've gotten into the building and Aunt Sookie's office. I normally have those doors locked."

Astor looked down. "I was here yesterday in the afternoon, helping Rachel with a class. She had to leave early to head back to the Pad. She didn't say why, so I told her I'll close up the school." He looked horrified for a second. "Could I have forgotten to lock the doors?" He ran his hands through is hair and started pacing. "I can't remember if I did, but I could have so they could easily have gotten in…" He shook his head. "I'm sorry, Summer. I must've forgotten. I'm so used to everyone doing things for me, that I'd forget to do something as simple and basic like locking doors when I leave."

The forlorn look on Astor's face made me want to comfort him instead of him comforting me. "It's okay, Astor. I'm alive and fine."

Astor hugged me close. "No, Summer, it's not fine. My actions caused you to get hurt. And God knows what he was doing in the office."

I frowned. 'I don't even want to know…"

"Well, I'm going to go check it out when I get the chance after this class, if this class gets started," Astor said.

I glanced over to the stage and my mouth fell opened. While Astor and I were talking, Drew had stepped up to the front of the class, and was leading them in warm up exercises.

"That's great!" he said. "Everyone's doing great! Now everyone gather together up close to the stage. I want to talk about characterization." He pointed at one of the students in class, a girl who was about fifteen, who blushed when Drew called her name. "Emma, what do you think characterization is?"

"Bringing qualities to a character in a story that makes him or her unique," she said, looking embarrassed.

Drew clapped. "Good description. That's part of it."

A bunch of hands went up, and Drew pointed at another student, a red-haired boy with glasses, about fourteen years old.

"It's making a character human," he said.

"Yes!" Drew said, "Give that guy a hand everyone!"

The class clapped, and Drew pointed at another student while Astor tugged at my hand. "Come on, Summer. Looks like Drew's got class covered. Let's see the damage this attacker did, and get a police report filed. So he's got battery, assault, trespassing…let's hope he doesn't add theft to that list, too."

I stared at Astor, "So when did you become good at all this crime terms?"

Astor laughed. "My next film in Vegas. Very stylish. I play a James Bond type of character who is a smooth Fader in the future, based on the dystopian book series, Fade, so I had to be familiar with what I was saying in the film. Have you heard of Sebastian Sorensen?"

"I've seen his name on the credits of some major films. Doesn't he compose music scores for the films?"

Astor nodded. "Yes, but he's also a producer. He's got a good eye for flair. The music score he composed for this film was amazing. He's producing this film, too. But..."

"What?" I asked. "Why are you grinning?"

"I heard he'll be guest teaching a drama class at USC this semester. I'm not a student, but I'd like to sit in on it, Summer. Would you like to take that class with me?"

"And be your bodyguard trying to keep all the girl students in class away from you?"

"No, they'll be too busy trying to get Professor Sorensen's attention. He was voted one of the Top Ten Sexiest Man in Hollywood."

I laughed. "So you're not threatened by that? I'm sure you made that list, too."

Astor smiled at me. "No, I can appreciate it, and it's something nice to be known as, but no, I'm not threatened by another man's looks. It's there, but men compare themselves in other ways besides looks. Unlike women."

"Exactly," I said. "It's too bad, it still boils down to that."

We had reached the door to the office, and I held my breath, prepared for the worst.

"Stay outside, Summer," he said. "I'll check it out first. Remember, they vandalized the place before and even attempted arson."

He walked in, and I heard him visibly cursed. That made me cringed.

"What?" I asked. "I'm coming in. Whatever it is…I can handle it."

Astor said, "No. You don't want to see this. It's disgusting."

"It can't be that bad…"

"No, Summer, You shouldn't come in here. Trust me…"

"Astor, it's my responsibility to take care of the Academy…"

"Summer…" Astor reached me right when I walked in and my jaw fell to the ground.

Perfect Summer (Loving Summer #2)

Astor tried frantically to erase the screen of the office computer, but it wouldn't shut off.

Besides seeing that all the files on the computer was wiped out, another pop up screen displayed a collage of photos...photos I didn't even know existed.

My life was displayed on screen. Even the most intimate photos, which I have no idea how and where it could have been taken. Clearly someone was obsessed. There were pictures of me running along the beach with Drew, photos of me at school, playing volleyball with my team, out at restaurants with Astor, one of me changing, one of me at the Academy walking to my car, one of me showering in the girl's locker room at high school, me on the beach passionately kissing Nat, me swimming in the pool at the Pad, then photos that made me want to vomit.

"Don't look, Summer," Astor said, pulling the plug on the computer.

The screen froze with the collage stuck onscreen, while the rest of the computer slowly shut down. The collage flashed on and off like a neon sign, as though it was there to taunt me. Too late, photos taken from the hospital where Aunt Sookie was cut open for her surgery was splashed across in the collage.

"What does this all mean?" I asked Astor.

"Come on, Summer," he said, grabbing me and dragging me away from the collage. "I don't know what it means, except this is no joke. I need to provide you with more security."

"Nat's already providing security," I said.

Astor looked angry. "Well, it's not enough, and…"

"No, I'm fine," I said. "I don't need a bodyguard with me all the time like you do."

"She's going to be fine," Drew's voice said firmly from behind us.

Astor scowled at Drew. "Look what happened to her today."

"That's because someone forgot to lock the doors," Drew said. He walked over to me and took my good hand. "Class just ended, Summer. I'll take you to the doctor's to get your arm checked."

Perfect Summer (Loving Summer #2)

"What about the budget and scheduling I have to do..." I said. Then I remembered how all the files were wiped out. "Oh, no..." I shook my head, realizing I have to start over from scratch.

Between the attack, seeing the collage, worrying about Drew, and now losing years of data from Aunt Sookie's computer; I finally broke down and cried.

Astor and Drew looked at each other, and I thought I saw a moment of understanding pass between them. "Look, Summer," Astor said, "Don't worry." He leaned over and kissed my forehead. "I'll take care of everything here. Go with Drew to the doctor's, and I'll call you with an update."

"Thanks," I said looking at Astor.

He brushed a strand of hair off my face, and looked like he wanted to kiss me, if it wasn't for Drew standing close by. "No need to thank me," he said. "I owe Aunt Sookie for all my success, Summer. I'm just trying to do what I can, especially if it means helping her gorgeous niece out."

There was a cough and a "please" heard from Drew's direction, and I hurriedly gave Astor a quick hug before turning to Drew.

We walked out of the Academy, and into the bright sunny daylight. I was about to take my SUV when Drew said, "You can't drive with your arm like that, Summer. How about I drive you to the doctor's. We'll take my car."

I was about to protest, but when we walked towards the midnight blue Lexus in the parking lot, I kept my mouth shut. This was one ride I didn't want to miss. Drew's car looked very familiar, although I swear I've never seen it before. As we got closer to the car, it finally dawn on me why it looked familiar. I had seen it before. Just last night. It was the one peeling away from the Pad's driveway last night after the passionate visit from my so-called phantom lover.

So Drew denied being at the Pad last night?

I wanted to prove he was wrong.

Chapter 5

It didn't take long to take x-rays of my arm and to determine I had fractured my elbow. The doctor, who happened to have been the Donovans' personal physician when they were living in Los Angeles, was a no-nonsense grandpa-like doctor who immediately put me at ease. We were in and out of his office within an hour with a wrapped elbow in a sling and two heated pads pressed against my bruised hips.

"Best doctor in town," Drew said driving me back to the Academy to get my car, "I missed him when we moved up to San Fran. Now it looks as though he'll be my physician again since I'm back."

I couldn't hide my smile. "Drew," I said. "I'm so happy you're back." I reached over to take his hand, but he seemed reluctant to take it at first until I traced my thumb on it affectionately. "Summer," he said, barely a whisper, "I wish you wouldn't do that."

"What?" I asked genuinely confused.

"Touch me," Drew said.

"I'm just trying to hold your hand," I said. "That's all. Nothing else."

Drew took a deep breath in and said, "Even that makes me want to jump you and make love to you from the time the sun rises to the time it sets."

"I'm sorry," I said, taking my hand away from his, but feeling more aroused than before.

Drew looked over at me, his blue eyes dark with desire. "It's okay, Summer. You can't help it. You can't help being such a loving person. That's your nature, just like I can't help being driven by a strong sex drive."

"Maybe that's why I like touching you," I said innocently.

Drew's eyes grew darker as his tongue darted out to lick the corners of his lips. It was a simple gesture, but so sexy I wanted to unbuckle my seatbelt, climb over to him, and ride his lap while kissing his luscious lips. "Summer, you don't realize how incredibly enticing that sounds," Drew said.

"I do," I answered back huskily. "I do realize how that can sound to you." I leaned back into my seat, fighting the temptation to unbuckle my seatbelt and play out the fantasy I had growing in back of my mind with Drew. "But do you realize," I said, "that maybe, just maybe, I might be the one with the strong sex drive, and you're the loving one. We just haven't explored those sides of us as fully as the other?"

Drew laughed then. "Maybe we should explore those sides of us more. I'd like to tell you to explore your strong sexual side with me, but that would move us pass the friend zone."

I looked down, remembering what Drew had told me about wanting to be just friends and nothing more. "Drew…" I said, "You really meant that about us being just friends?"

Drew kept staring straight ahead, but his jaw noticeably twitched. Even that made me want to reach out and touch his jaw.

"Yes," Drew said. "We can't cross the boundaries, Summer. Or someone will get hurt. It's like the whole casual sex thing. Both parties know what they're getting into from the beginning. Just pure sex and nothing else."

"So with us, our boundaries are just pure friendship, platonic friendship and nothing else?" I asked.

Drew turned his head to look at me before looking at the road again. "It's one way or another, Summer. For me, it's black and white. You're either in the friend zone or the lover zone. And with you...Gosh, Summer, you're in my danger zone. My rip-my-heart-out and change-me-forever zone. I have to tread lightly with you. Because if I don't, I may never be able to find my way back."

Drew stopped the car, and parked it at the Academy lot. By now, everyone had left, even Astor, and the lot was empty except for my lone SUV.

I didn't know what I could say to him.

Perfect Summer (Loving Summer #2)

"Look, Summer," Drew said, "there are a million things I want to say to you. There are a million things I want to do to you right now. None of them are in the friend zone at the moment. If I don't drop you off now here at a neutral place, I would be crossing the friend zone into the danger zone."

"Understood," I said.

Drew looked over at me. He looked determined. "As much as I love the Pad, as much as I want to move there, I'm staying in an apartment closer to USC, Summer. I'll have to be on campus a lot for football practice, and it made sense for me to live closer."

"Will I get to see you at all then?" I asked.

"I'll still come out to help out with the Academy, Summer, and when you need me. We're still friends…only we won't be living under the same roof like at the Pad."

"Okay," I said. "That's fine with me, friend." I looked away from Drew, not wanting him to see how hurt I felt. I knew it was the best way to handle everything between us, but I still couldn't help feeling sad.

Drew got out of the car and came over to open the door for me. He helped me into my car, and gently kissed my forehead. "I'm glad you're alright, Summer. You've had quite a day so just go home and rest, like Dr. Williams told you to. Rachel's at the Pad with you for at least tonight so I know you're not alone. And my apartment is just a few miles away. If you need anything, call me."

"Thank you, Drew," I said looking up at him. "For everything." My lips trembled with the emotions I was holding back. I felt as though we were stepping back, that Drew was pushing me away, keeping me at a distance now more than ever. But he was right. I couldn't give him more. I couldn't give him what he wanted from me in order to get him past the danger zone.

"See you on campus," Drew said, walking back to his car.

"Sure," I said, starting my car, and backing up. "See you on campus. Have a great first week, if I don't see you."

Drew nodded, and I took off, not looking back. If I did, and he saw me, he would have seen the big fat tears that started rolling down my cheeks.

It wasn't so much that I felt like I had lost a closeness with Drew that had developed all last summer, but it was also the same feeling of lost I felt when the Donovans had moved away to San Francisco, leaving me behind with Aunt Sookie.

I hated that feeling of abandonment. Drew had moved closer to me only to move emotionally away. Rachel was going to go back home to San Francisco for another semester before she would be back to help out with summer classes at the Academy and to try to start acting professionally with Astor's help. Astor was back, but only for a short time before he would leave for a film shoot in Vegas.

I was all alone again. But this time, I didn't even have Aunt Sookie.

My phone began ringing, and I put on my earpiece to talk hands free while driving. "Hello?"

"Summer," Nat's voice flowed through to me in a soothing tone. "I heard about what happened at the Academy today. Rachel sent me word, and then I even got a message from Drew. The first one since we started looking for him. I didn't even know you found him, that he was there with you. Why didn't you tell me? Never mind, I'm coming down tonight to see you."

"But you have work and your school's starting soon, too."

"This is more important, Summer. You're more important. You know how I felt that we can't be together because of the distance and my obligations…well, that's a lot of crock. I realized it this morning having breakfast with you. I'd do anything and everything to be with you, Summer. I know you don't believe it, but I love you so much. I always have, and I'll see you tonight."

"I can't wait," I said.

"Me, too," Nat said. "Now get home and get some rest. You'll need it tonight, Summer. I'll take good care of you like you've never been taken cared of before."

Perfect Summer (Loving Summer #2)

My entire body tingled, remembering about Nat and how skillful he was in bed. "Promised?" I asked.

"Promised," Nat said before we both ended the call.

*****

That night, Nat made good on his promise.

Right after Rachel left with Ryan to fly back on the Donovan's corporate jet, Nat led me to the sofa where he gently and slowly undressed me, kissing me as he went along. We spent the entire night, exploring each other's bodies, and I was lost, completely enveloped by Nat's skillful lovemaking.

Without worrying about whether or not we'll hurt Drew by being together like this, the intensity in our lovemaking grew tenfold. Despite how sad I felt about Drew, part of me felt happy and exhilarated for now making a clear decision on Drew. He wanted only friendship. Nothing more. So he had set me free to be with anyone I wanted.

And there was only one other man I wanted badly besides Drew.

Nat.

Nat wanted me badly too. It was as though he had been holding back the entire time before, but it was different this time.

"Summer," he said, tenderly kissing the tip of my breasts before moving down to kiss my stomach. "I want you to know how much I love you. There's no holding back anymore. When I heard about you being attacked, how you were hurt, I've never wanted to hurt someone so much. I wanted to find that asshole who did this to you. Who touched you, who ransacked the Academy's office and tried to mind fuck you, too. I wanted to kill him. But Drew called me and said he did a number on him at the theater. Astor was able to find out more about the guy who broke into the office when he filed a police report. He actually called Donovan Dynamics to ask for help to trace and find out more about the guy. Drew called too, about wanting to find the guy and make sure he'd never hurt you again.

Drew also told me a lot. About how he felt that night he visited my apartment, and how he's stepping back."

Nat stopped kissing me and moved up to look at me in the eyes. "Summer, it's your choice, who you want to be with. As long as you're happy. That's what mattered to Drew and me. But until you can decide, Drew's stepped back and started moving on. I can't say the same for me, because I just couldn't. And based on how much I felt when I heard about your attack, and how much I realized I shouldn't waste any more time wondering what could have been, but acting on what I want the most right now, I realized you're the one thing I wanted the most. When I took you to see the Donovan Den, I realized I was miserable living there all those years because you weren't there. When you went there with me that night, being there with you negated all the miserable feelings. I started liking the place again. Because of you, Summer."

He kissed me hard and kept holding my face in his hands. "Summer, I want you with me all the time. I want us to be together, but at the same time, I know I can't be here with you all the time...physically and because of the distance. I wish I can, and maybe someday soon, I can, but in the meantime, I want you safe. Astor and I talked about getting you a bodyguard, but thought you wouldn't go for that. You're so independent. But if we're wrong about that, Donovan Dynamics can offer you one."

"No," I said, "I wouldn't want a bodyguard."

"So, the solution is for you to learn to protect yourself. Take self-defense classes, even maybe carry a gun or a weapon, like pepper spray or stun gun, and have it registered with the authorities. We just don't want you defenseless against guys like Sloane."

"Sloane?" I asked. "Is that the name of the guy who attacked me and nearly raped me?"

"Stanley Sloane," Nat said. "A loner in his thirties. Been collecting pictures of you for a while. We think he may have been obsessed with Aunt Sookie, too." Nat paused. "Sookie was a beauty like you when she first appeared in films. She even had a massive fan following when she starred as the comic book heroine Red Phoenix, in that short-lived television show Masters of the Universe.

Perfect Summer (Loving Summer #2)

Sloane was found in forums talking about comic books, and how Red Phoenix played by Sookie Jones was one of the sexiest heroines ever on television. He may have been a little obsessed with her, and in a lot of ways, you kinda look like her. Many of those photos of you in the showers or on the beach, even that one of us kissing…they were taken with a telephoto lens from far away. We're still trying to piece together who Sloane is, does he work for anyone, and how did he have access to some of those private records…hospital reports, Aunt Sookie's stuff."

"Probably stolen it," I said. "He broke into the school and tampered with the Academy's computer, wiping away the files," I said. "I wouldn't put it pass him to have broken into, even hacked his way into some private records."

"Precisely," Nat said. "But don't worry, we can find stuff on him too, and hacking into private records like that is criminal with stiff penalties."

I shuddered, remembering how I felt lying on the ground with Sloane on top of me, rubbing against me, his grubby dirty hands over my mouth to keep me from screaming as his other hand fumbled with my underwear, trying to pull it down. It was horrifying and wrong. I wanted none of that, an act of trying to make me feel helpless and small. Thank God for Drew…

"I'm going to take martial arts classes as soon as I can," I told Nat. "I don't want to fall victim like that again."

"Good," Nat said, kissing my forehead. "I'll help you find a good school to train at."

"I'll look into pepper sprays, too," I said. "It doesn't hurt to be prepared."

"No, it doesn't," Nat agreed. "I just wished I can be here in Malibu with you all the time to protect you…"

I saw the tender look of love in his eyes and knew he was still worried about me. "I know that's impossible right now," I said. "I wished that could happen, too, but for right now, I'll have to be the one protecting myself."

Nat traced my lips with his fingers before pressing his lips on mine. "You can, Summer. Everyone has the right to protect themselves. If Drew never had gotten to the theater on time, I don't even want to think what could've happened. You struggling and fighting back against Sloane most likely deterred him - buying you time before someone showed up. So, Summer. Your safety goes beyond any jealousies we have over you. Astor, Drew, and me. It's no secret guys are all over the place with you, that they're crazy about you. We're all trying to compete for you, in a barbaric caveman way that's part of our DNA so we're going to be jealous of each other. But in a way, if it means you're being protected and not alone, then we'd set aside any jealousy for you to be safe."

"What are you saying?" I asked.

"I'm not going to be around every day. Astor has a grueling work and travel schedule. That leaves Drew. He's at least here and have the most stable schedule. If you need him around just so you're not alone, you have my blessing."

"Nat," I said, overwhelmed by his love. "You're fine with Drew staying over and spending that much time with me?"

"I don't like it, but I don't like you getting attacked by some Slone guy even more."

Nat got up to shower and get dressed. I watched his naked chiseled muscular body move with grace and confidence to the bathroom I shared with Rachel. He was breathtakingly hot, and I thought about joining him in the showers. Since starting college and keeping a disciplined work-out schedule, Nat had gotten into top shape. Though not as broad as Drew, Nat had the sexy body of a quarterback, and the stamina of a racehorse. We packed a full day of passion last night into a few hours...which should have left us satisfied. Instead it left me wanting me.

I sighed. *Ain't going to happen today.* He wouldn't get a chance to spend the entire day with me because he needed to be back in San Francisco, starting a new semester at Stanford tomorrow, taking care of his mother, and working at Donovan Dynamics. I was happy to finally reach a point in our relationship where he was willing to try to be together, despite all the demons he faced.

Perfect Summer (Loving Summer #2)

It was what I had always wanted since our first kiss. He had become the pirate to my princess, who was going to defy all odds for us to be together. I should have been happy. I should have been satisfied, but deep down inside, why did I still have my doubts he would become the knight who swept me off my feet to a land of happily ever after?

Chapter 6

My first week of college started off with a bang. Because I was starting school in the last semester of college, rather than the first like most freshmen, I had to adjust quickly to a new school, new schedule, and college life. Winter break was done, and everyone had gone back to school. Rachel had left a couple of days ago, while Nat had returned to San Francisco just a day ago.

Entering college was a whole new world for me, which was both exciting, yet scary. Being a new girl without a single classmate from the same school as mine, meaning no friends, being a new recruit on the college volleyball team, and just joining in during the middle of the school year left me floundering and grasping to catch up.

Perfect Summer (Loving Summer #2)

My first days were spent getting lost, trying to find study groups to join, and frantically trying to catch up on assignments many students who had taken a prior class last semester had already had a head start completing before the Winter Break. I only had four classes for the semester, but it felt like five since one of them, my English Literature and Drama one, had a separate class or lab, as it was called, that met once a week. With Aunt Sookie's Academy starting a Spring program, college, and me fumbling around with my good arm in a cast, I was literally feeling handicapped and overwhelmed.

The assignments were a lot more work than the one in high school, and I had underestimated the amount of time I needed to complete them, causing me to spend the first few days studying far into the night and getting very little sleep.

By the end of the week, I was exhausted, but more confident about college, as I head over to the last class of the week, English Literature and Drama, which was held in a room the size of an auditorium. With no assigned seats, I headed for the back of the auditorium where there were a few seats left and sat next to a girl with dark shoulder-length hair and brown eyes, wearing a red USC sweatshirt and jeans. As soon as I sat down, she handed me a sheet of paper.

"Thanks," I said, looking at it. It was a blank piece of paper with names and phone numbers on there. "Um, what is this for?"

The girl blew a bubble with her chewing gum, and said, "It's the sign-up sheet for the lab. It's like another class, only smaller where we get into groups to read and discuss the books that we're reading in class."

"A reading group?" I asked.

"Mostly a study group, but if you like what we're reading, yeah, kinda like a reading club, only we go over some discussion questions that we think will be on the exams."

"Why is this a class?" I asked. "Do you get credit for this?"

"No credit," the girl said, "but it's popular because most of the time, whatever the group studies and discuss in the group, is found on the exams."

"So it's a way for us to find a study group to belong to," I said.

"Yes," the girl said. "Believe me, you would want to be in this group. Professor Standish's exams are ridiculously hard. Many college careers and dreams of getting a high grade point average in college were derailed by a poor grade from this class."

"Oh," I said, hastily adding my name and number to the list. "Thank you for telling me all this…"

"Trish," the girl said, extending her hand. "My brother took this class, and to this day, he swore it was the toughest class he's ever had."

"Literature and Drama?" I asked. "How can that be so tough?"

Trish's eyes opened wide. "Glad you're pretty confident about that, um…"

"Summer," I said.

"Summer," Trish said. "Professor Standish teaches this class like it's a doctoral program instead of an undergraduate class. He's one of the leading authorities on classical plays. Many of the things taught here aren't even known yet, and Standish is about to publish an anthology of classical critiques analyzing the role of plays on society throughout civilizations."

"Okay," I said. "You've got me convinced to take good notes."

"And never fall asleep in class. This is a big class, and you think you can hide behind the masses, but he always manage to find that one student who isn't paying attention or have fallen asleep to ask the hardest question. If you answer wrong, then he makes sure to subtract a point from your exam."

"It doesn't help this class is way early in the morning," I said.

"That's why he does this...almost half the class is barely awake for class."

Perfect Summer (Loving Summer #2)

"Smart," I laughed. "I should try that for my evening scene classes." I made a note to myself, and added in bold script, DRINK COFFEE.

I got up from my seat to walk over a few seats to the next student at the end of my row with the group sign-up sheet, and was about to head back to my seat when I spotted a familiar jersey on one of the students sitting in front.

He was a large guy with dark, almost black wavy hair that was cropped close to his head, wearing a San Francisco 49er jersey which was filled out by broad shoulders, and talking animatedly with the pretty blonde girl seated to his right. On his left was a bosomy brunette, pressed close to him, acting very interested in what he was saying. Clearly the best-looking guy in class, based on the view from behind, he seemed to carry himself with easy confidence and charisma. Girls seemed to be drawn to him from left to right. Even behind him was a row of well-manicured, well-made up nicely dress girls leaning forward towards him, as though they wanted to hear what he said.

At one point, they all burst out laughing, and one of the girls in back, patted his shoulders, which got his attention.

Boy, I thought I'd seen it all before with good-looking cocky guys using their looks and body to get sex, casual sex whenever they wanted it, but all that flirtation right in front of class…it was shameful how the women were throwing themselves at him. One of them was playing with his hair even, and another had leaned in to whisper into his ear, while touching his neck from behind.

I was about to head back to my seat when he turned around abruptly, as though he had heard someone call his name. Without hesitation, his blue eyes traveled up to the back of the room where it met mine. For a second, my breath caught in my throat, and I was frozen in place, staring down into eyes I've seen several times over the years. Drew's.

He had an easy smile on his face when he first turned around, but when his eyes met mine, his smile disappeared, and a look of pain briefly flickered on his face, causing a couple of the girls to turn around to see what could've caused Mr. Hot and Perfect to get serious for a second.

I quickly made my way back to my seat before the girls could recognize me standing there, and began flipping through my notebook. I should've recognized Drew from the start, but his new haircut, clean and closely cropped, threw me off.

Him surrounded by so many girls, threw me off. Apparently, he had no problem adjusting to college life so soon, unlike me.

I felt more pathetic thinking about how challenging this first week of school was for me, than it was for him. How at ease he seemed talking to obviously the most prettiest and popular girls who looked like they just walked out of a salon, on campus while I was dressed in an old grey Twilight t-shirt, cut-off jeans, and a long white cotton cardigan and sneakers, looking like some high school nerd while he looked like some hot underwear model.

Stop feeling so insecure!

My brain was trying to get me to focus, while I struggled to put aside my feelings. It must be the lack of sleep, having my arm in a sling, and missing my friends and Aunt Sookie.

Luckily, I didn't have time to dwell on my sudden feeling of insecurity, as Trish nudged me with her elbow.

The class grew silent, and a man in his fifties walked to the podium. He had stark white hair that stood up like a lion's mane, and a nicely trimmed beard that was a shade of salt and pepper like his moustache.

For an older man, he was striking, dressed entirely in black. Instantly my eyes were riveted to his commanding distinguished presence. He looked, acted, and embodied the very essence of what I had imagined a professor of drama and literature would be.

He turned on the screen behind him, and took out a clipper-like device. Then he talked into the microphone in front of him. "In case you think this class is the Tribal Storytelling Through the Ages Class, I'm Professor Standish, and this is Classical Literature and Drama"

Perfect Summer (Loving Summer #2)

So he had a dry sense of humor, I thought. I was already beginning to like the class, even though Drew was in it, too, with his harem of Mrs. Drew wannabes.

Having Drew in the same class as me shouldn't be so bad. After all, it was what we had originally planned when we both heard we were going to start school a semester earlier. But plans change, and now it seemed old Drew was back, along with his full Drew Effect.

It shouldn't bother me so much. It wasn't as though we were together. It wasn't as though we have a commitment to each other. Somehow, however, just seeing him up there flirting with those girls, letting them touch him, and even shamelessly give him their numbers; I felt sick to my stomach.

I wanted to ignore him, to forget he was here, but that was impossible. In order to pay attention in class and follow along Professor Standish's lecture, I had to stare straight in the direction of Drew and harem to Professor Standish. Having him in the line of sight to the professor was the most distracting thing I've ever experienced in class. My eyes were riveted to the girls next to Drew, lightly playing with his hair or even rubbing his back.

At times, Drew would look over at one of them and whisper into her ears or lean playfully into another. Except for that one time he turned back and made eye contact with me, he acted like he didn't know me.

He didn't even glance back at me once as the lecture slowly ended. By then, I was fuming mad. I wanted to run out of there and head straight home. Maybe go jogging on the beach, to get that image of him and those girls out of my head.

Professor Standish finished his lecture, and I bolted out of my seat so fast, I knocked over my textbook, and bag, making everything spill to the ground with a loud thump. Everyone in front of me, including Professor Standish turned to look in my direction, as I bent down and tried unsuccessfully to pick up my books, pens, hairbrush, and phone. With one arm in a sling, I was sure I made an awkward sight.

Trish bent down to help me, and I whispered a quick "Thank You".

"No problem," she said. "It must be tough enough having to carry all those books and everything with a broken arm."

"I can manage," I said, almost finished picking up a small first aid kit.

I was reaching for my small turquoise leather notepad, which Nat had jotted down a sweet note in, when a large hand reached over and plucked it up off the floor.

Still crouching on the ground with Trish next to me, I followed that hand up long muscular legs clad in tight jeans up an obvious smooth washboard stomach, well-defined chest, shoulders, and arms, to a handsome chiseled face with blue eyes and dark hair.

Drew. He looked angry, but he didn't say anything except stare at me as though he wanted to shake me.

I bit my lips, trying to keep from letting out a frustrated sigh. Finally, he acknowledged me in class like this?

Trish saw the looks Drew and I exchanged each other as though we were about to start a duel and excuse herself. "Well, I'll see you in the group study on Monday," she said. "Good luck with things, Summer."

"Thanks!" I cracked a smile. Looks like I may have made a new friend in college.

Drew flipped the cover of my notepad over, glanced at what was written inside, and visibly clenched his jaw tighter.

I didn't want to wait to see why he was so pissed at me. I placed the strap of my bag over my shoulders, and brushed past him, on my way out of the classroom without turning back.

I was about a few steps away from exit when a hand grabbed my good elbow from behind. "Summer, wait," Drew said.

I stopped to glare at him. "What do you want?"

Drew ran his hand through his hair, and bit his lips. His eyes darted all over my face, resting on my eyes and mouth a couple of times. "Summer," he said, a note of longing in his voice.

I tried crossing my arms, but my sling got in the way so I ended up using my good hand to hold the forearm of my bad arm. When I found a comfortable and less awkward position, I stopped fumbling and waited for Drew to say what he had to say.

"Summer..." he began and stopped. He finally handed me my notepad, saying, "You dropped this."

I took it and said, "Thanks. Nat gave that to me before he left for San Fran."

Drew nodded. "I know. It's Nat's notepad. I've seen it hundreds of times. It was a gift from Aunt Sookie years ago when he turned ten."

"Oh," I said, vaguely remembering the details.

Drew shuffled on his feet. "So you and Nat..." he didn't finished.

"Drew..." I said being as gentle as I could. "Nat and I are close. You kinda pushed me closer to him, Drew."

He looked down then, and said, "Yeah, I did."

"So, don't look at me like that, Drew."

"Like what?"

"Like you want to kiss me, but strangle me at the same time." I took a step closer to him and touched his cheeks with my hand. "Why are you so angry at me?"

"Summer," Drew closed his eyes and leaned his cheek into my hand. "Oh, Summer," he said. "How I missed you."

I didn't say anything for a while, but stepped closer, close enough to smell his familiar spicy vanilla scent. He smelled so sexy, I want to lean further into him, to rest my hands and face on his chest and be held by him.

Instead, I looked up into his eyes, and asked. "Why didn't you contact me this week, Drew? You knew I was also starting college this week with you…"

Drew shot me an angry look. "You could've contacted me, too, Summer. Why didn't you want to see me?" He looked hurt and angrier than before. "Is it because of Nat?"

"No, of course not, Drew. I would never forget you just because Nat and I are closer, but I…I had to catch up with everything, it was so overwhelming, I didn't think…"

"It was hard on me, too, the first day," Drew said. "But it got easier, and I ended up meeting a lot of people…"

"I know," I said. "I saw all those girls around you."

Drew cracked a grin as wide as the sky then. "It doesn't stop, even here in college."

"The Drew Effect…" I smiled back.

Drew nodded. "Only they attack in numbers…sorority sisters here. They love the new football players."

"No," I said, "they love you."

Drew closed his mouth and opened it again, swallowing his surprise. "I only care to hear those words from one girl, Summer, and you know pretty much who she is."

He was staring at my mouth then, and cupped my chin in his hand.

"Drew…" I said. "Why don't you come over to the Pad tonight for dinner? It'll be like old times, and we can go for a swim, jog, even cook together."

Drew's eyebrows lifted, and he said gruffly. "Is that all that's going to happen?"

"I don't know," I said. "That's what I intend to happen, but…"

"You don't know me very well then, Summer," Drew said.

"Why?" I said. "I think I do."

"If you do, then you would know that to invite me over for dinner, a swim, and even a jog along the beach just us two alone at the Pad…" Drew's eyes had grown darker with desire as he looked into mine, trying to convey his meaning without saying it. "If we're honest with ourselves…we both know that couldn't happen." He leaned in to whisper into my ears. "The way I'm feeling right now, if you get me alone in a room with you, I'd tear off every piece of clothing on you, and make love to you all night, all weekend."

I blushed, thinking about it.

"No, Summer," Drew said softly. "As much as I want to visit and stay with you at the Pad, I have to say no.

"No?" I asked.

"No," Drew said, turning away from me and stepping back. "I can't trust myself to refrain from touching you, Summer. It's too tempting."

"But we're friends," I said.

"Exactly," Drew replied. "You're a friend I want to fuck. But I need you to be just a friend. It's best to remain that."

Drew picked up his bag from the floor, and slung it over his shoulders. "I'll see you around, Summer. Take care."

Then he was gone.

*****

I never thought I'd feel so sad about Drew wanting to just be friends with me. My mind and heart refused to believe it, reliving all the things and actions he'd ever said and done for me.

Kailin Gow

I guess I thought that I'd always have him around, that I'll always have his love.

Being at Aunt Sookie's at night without anyone around, having had an exhausting first week of school, and still reeling from my near rape attack; I felt so alone.

I decided to try to get Drew to come out again, for pizza and maybe to study a little, but when I called him at his apartment, an unfamiliar girl's voice picked up the phone, giggling.

"Is Drew there?" I asked.

"Oh, you mean the football hottie?" the girl asked.

"I guess so," I said, rolling my eyes.

"He's busy at the moment," she said, giggling. What? Was she drunk or something?

"Well, when he's not 'busy'," I said. "Can you tell him to call Summer?"

"Why?" the girl asked. "So you can jump in line ahead of the rest of us? Take a number, Summer," the girl said. "He's going to be busy with the squad tonight. And sore..." she giggled.

Perfect Summer (Loving Summer #2)

"Urghh," I hung up, not wanting to hear more disgusting things from that girl's mouth.

I went to my freezer and pulled out a pint of caramel coffee ice cream and grabbed a spoon. What happened to the Drew I knew and began falling in love with? Yes, in love…like in love with Nat in love. Why was he with all those girls? Why did he have to have them?

I planted my pint of ice cream in front of me, and took out my textbooks. Why should I care if he was with them or any girl? He and I weren't dating. We weren't together. We were just friends. And if he was back to his manwhoring bad boy ways, then that was his choice.

But as I dipped my spoon into the ice cream over and over again, I felt my heart sinking with each bite.

As much as I understood why he was with those girls, and why he was avoiding me, I hated it, especially the white hot jealousy I felt, wanting to drive over to Drew's apartment to tear each girl off of him.

People, I bet think I would be lucky having the love of these two wonderful guys. I was very lucky. Only why did I feel miserable being in love with two guys who both meant so much to me? If I chose one, I'd lose the other…and not just a lover, but one of my best friends.

I didn't want to fall in love, but I did…first with Nat a long time ago, and then with Drew over the course of last summer. Love had no expirations. It couldn't be shut off just like that. Even if I tried, I knew I couldn't stop loving them both.

Chapter 7

I didn't have time to be upset about Drew. That night, I fell asleep reading one of the textbooks at the kitchen table, and didn't wake up until early morning the next day.

My face was resting on my Microeconomics textbook when I heard a creak next to me. I opened my eyes to find Nat sitting beside me, watching me sleep. When my eyes opened wider, he pulled up closer and kissed me on my cheeks. "Hi Beautiful," he said. "I've been enjoying watching you sleep."

"That can be boring," I said.

"Not when I'm looking at someone so beautiful I can stare at all day."

I laughed. "That's kind of creepy stalker behavior."

Nat laughed and placed his hands on my back, kneading it, massaging it, and applying pressure where I needed it.

"Oh, that feels so good, Nat," I groaned. "I so need this!"

"I figured," Nat said. "You've had quite a week, I'm sure, Summer. And I want to hear all about it."

"Let's just say I didn't have a good of a time starting college than Drew did."

Nat raised his eyebrows. "Really? Why?"

"He plays the role of football hero to the t, doesn't he?" I said. "

"He's been known to," Nat said.

"Well, turns out he's in the same Literature and Drama class as me on Fridays, and he was, as always, surrounded by girls."

"Doesn't surprise me," Nat said smiling. "Drew will be Drew."

"But I thought he'd changed. I thought he'd given that all up…"

Nat stopped smiling. "Summer, I know you know how Drew felt about you, but sometimes people change, and well, I think Drew was really hurt by seeing us together, but instead of being consumed by it, he's moved on."

I tried to keep the hurt I felt from showing, knowing that Drew was serious about just being friends and nothing more. I didn't want Nat to know how much I cared, especially since it was Nat I've always had a crush on for years, not Drew.

"I have to admit, Summer," Nat said. "Drew's got more backbone than he'd led on. I thought he would do something stupid and maybe even dangerous at first, out of crazy jealousy, but he turned everything around. Set aside his feelings, faced reality, and moved on. He even sent me a text after Donovan Dynamics found him saying that he was fine, not to worry. He just needed to get his head straight and figure things out. After driving for a while, he realized what he had for you was more a childhood crush than lasting love."

I wanted to bolt out of my seat and into my room to be alone then, but Nat continued on. "He gave us his blessing to see each other." Nat patted my shoulders and held my hand. "Without the guilt that we may hurt him, Summer. He only wished us happiness."

"But..." I blurted out. "I never got to talk to him about all that. I never wanted to hurt him."

"He knows, Summer," Nat said. "But he also didn't want to stand in the way of us being together, if we were meant to be." Nat pursed his lips. "I'm proud and amazed at how Drew has been acting. He's become a great guy with a good head on his shoulders."

I couldn't agree more, and decided to do the same as Drew: move on. Nat was here, and I didn't want to waste any time worrying about what could've been and what should've. Aunt Sookie had taught me to live in the moment, to embrace everything life had to offer. Now, Nat was here, and I knew he wanted me as much as I wanted him so I put a brave face forward, and made the most of Nat's visit. I did have so much to share with Nat. I wanted to talk to him about college, about my classes, and everything else besides Drew...

"College is," I started. "A lot more than I expected, I'll be honest. It's a lot more work than high school, but I love learning everything I've signed up for. The professors are fascinating, and I love the autonomy of being able to determine how well I do, just based on putting the effort in."

Nat laughed. "Already sounding like a college-educated woman, Summer." He kissed the top of my head from behind as he moved closer to begin applying harder strokes and pressure on my back. "But, you need to take it easier on yourself, baby. Your back is as stiff as a board."

He led me to the area in front of the fireplace where a large fluffy sheepskin rug was placed, and had me lay out on my stomach. "This will give me more leverage on your back than you leaning on the kitchen table. Now close your eyes and relax."

I closed my eyes just as Nat went over to the windows and closed the blinds. He started up some soothing music in the background, and I even started smelling the sweet scent of jasmine, lavender, and vanilla. Before I knew it, Nat was back and placed his warmed and oiled hands on the skin of my back, massaging up, slowly and sensually.

He turned me around, took the hem of my t-shirt, and rolled it off of me, exposing my naked breasts. Nat growled. "No bra. That was a nice surprise, Summer."

"It's far more comfortable that way," I said.

"And accessible," Nat said, bending down to take one of my harden nipples in his mouth.

"Oh Nat," I moaned. "What happened to the massage?"

Nat's tongue circled around my orb and then slowly licked the tip. When it grew harder, he increased the pressure and speed of his tongue on my nipple until I wanted to explode.

Perfect Summer (Loving Summer #2)

But he held back from letting me, instead, turning his skillful mouth to my other breast, lavishing the same attention to it as the other. I was writhing in pleasure, asking him to give me more, when his hands unbuttoned the top of my jeans shorts, unzipped it, and pulled it down. Free from the any stitch of clothing, his hot hands reached up and began rubbing, stroking my heated folds.

He moved his lips from my breasts to kiss the center of my ribs and make his way down my stomach, belly button, and pelvic bone.

I buckled underneath him as all of my senses were filled with need for him. "Nat," I moaned. "I. Need. You."

"Hold on a little bit more, baby," Nat said, lifting my legs up on his shoulders as he bent his head lower. "Trust me, this will only make the massage easier…"

"You're so practical, Nat…" I began, but nearly jump out of my skin when his cool wet tongue touched me and began pushing into me. It took my breath away how good it felt. But then he was relentless in his onslaught on me, using his hands, his mouth, his tongue, and even is massive hard-on to the point of intense release.

When the intense waves of pleasure stopped rocking my entire body, I stretched out fully on the rug, gazing up into Nat's sea green eyes. "I feel like jello," I said.

"Not yet," Nat smiled, kissing me passionately on my lips, while taking my lower lips between his lips to suck and chew on.

"Oh," I cried, feeling my body respond to his kiss with renewed energy. "You're still not through?"

Nat grinned between his onslaught of my mouth. "No, Summer. I don't think I can get enough of you. An entire week without being able to touch, hold, and kiss you, is a lifetime for me. I'm just catching up."

He sat up and turned me forward so I was on my stomach. "Now let's work your back."

He started off using his hands to knead and stroke my back, then began kissing the back of my neck and shoulders as his hands touched and stroked the curve of my lower back, my hips, and then my butt.

Perfect Summer (Loving Summer #2)

"Summer," he said huskily. "You have the most perfect body I've ever seen. I can touch and kiss you all day and still not get enough of you." He kissed my hips, and palmed my butt cheeks. Then went on his knees, pulling me up on my hands and knees by the waist. "Summer," he said. "Do you want me?" His fingers stroked my inner thighs.

"Yes," I groaned. "I want you now."

"How much?" he asked.

"All the way," I said. "You've always wanted me, was always good to me, good for me. Why shouldn't I want you, Nat?"

"Are you sure?" Nat asked.

"Yes," I said, not able to think straight with his fingers moving against me, in me, and causing all kinds of heated sensations deep from the core of me.

"Good," Nat said, his voice choked up yet full of desire. "I want you so badly, it hurts. I want you so much I can't think of anything else. You are my stars and sky, Summer. I love you so much!" With that he drove into me from behind, causing me to almost fall flat on my face.

With a passion neither of us knew we had for each other, we kept going, he kept pleasuring me, until we couldn't tell if it was morning, noon, or night.

*****

Nat spent the entire weekend with me, cooking for me, running with me on the beach, and making love to me at night.

He left Monday morning to fly back to San Francisco, but left me with a charm bracelet he brought me from Tiffany's. It was filled with little charms already – a starfish, a pirate ship, a princess crown, and a small heart. "It's to remember me when I'm not here, Summer," he said. "Now I have to go, but I'll call you tonight." He kissed me on top of my head and then on my lips before heading off.

Nat was everything I had always imagined him to be when he finally let down his guards and succumb to what he felt for me. He was perfect. He made me feel perfect when we were together…but why did I still feel incomplete?

Chapter 8

"Being with Nat like that kept me in a cloud for almost the entire week. He was so much sexier than I've ever imagine. Much more romantic than the responsible and no-nonsense Nat I've known for years. Finally doing the deed with him and losing my virginity to him brought me to a new awareness of myself as a woman and my needs as one. I realized now that Nat had truly grown up, become a man over the years, in more ways than one.

As I sat in Professor Standish's class, absently playing with my charm bracelet, I barely noticed Drew slipping into the seat next to me.

"Nice bracelet," Drew said, fingering it. "Looks like something Astor would get you…"

"No," I said. "Not from Astor. But that doesn't make it too expensive for me to accept, too. I might return it, but it would only hurt his feelings."

"Nat, then," Drew said unusually indifferently. "He doesn't hand out gifts like candy, Summer. If he gave you that charm bracelet as a gift, then it meant a lot to him that you accept it."

I nodded. "Thanks, Drew. I'll keep it then. I really like the thought and details he put into it more than anything." I showed him the pirate charm, the starfish, and even the princess one.

"Cute," Drew said drily. "Such attention to details. So very Nat."

I could hear the bit of jealousy hidden in his false cheerfulness and turned to him. "Drew, nice to see you back here for class. Why are you here sitting with me instead of up there with your harem?"

Drew turned serious eyes to me, and said, "Just wanted to see how you're doing. How's your arm?"

"Good," I said. "I'm doing great, and my arm..." I moved it a little, "it's healing...that's all I can say about that. I don't think there's anything else I could do to get it to heal faster."

Drew reached over to touch my arm, and a jolt of electric thrill went through me. He gently traced it from the top of my shoulder to my fingertips. "How does that feel?"

"I can feel it, at least," I said. "A few days ago, it still felt numb, but today…"

Drew smiled his megawatt smile. "You feel as good as new!"

"Why do you say that?" I asked, looking suspiciously at him.

"Because I can see, no, I can tell, things have gotten much better since the first week of school for you."

"How observant," I said. "I barely saw you since last Friday. How could you tell just from looking at me now?"

Drew's eyes darted to the side and down before facing me again. "Just because you don't see me, Summer, doesn't mean I'm not around."

I narrowed my eyes at him. "What do you mean by that?"

Drew ran his hand through his hair and muttered, "Shoot, I shouldn't have said that."

"What are you talking about?" I asked. I turned my body to face him, giving him my full attention. "What's going on?"

"Just that, although we're not in the same classes together except for this one, and just because I don't come over to the Pad to stay with you, doesn't mean I haven't been looking out for you, Summer. Making sure you're safe."

"You have?" My eyes must've gotten as big as saucers, looking at him incredulously. "Why?"

"Because I want to," Drew said. "I want to make sure the guy who attacked you won't be able to again."

"But why all the secret agent stuff?" I asked.

Drew looked very uncomfortable then. "Because Summer, I shouldn't be with you." He took a deep breath, "but I try to watch after you, making sure when you leave your classes at night throughout the week, that you make it to your car safely."

"Wow," I said, "I didn't know...I'm sorry if I sounded snarky earlier...it just seems like you wanted to avoid me this entire time..."

"I would never want that, Summer," Drew said, looking wistfully at my face.

"But why do you have to keep your distance from me, why can't you see me, talk to me like a real person...like Drew, not some kind of distant non-friend."

"Non-friend?" Drew smiled drily at my choice of words. "I like the sound of that better than 'friends', Summer. It probably describes us best."

"And what are we?" I asked, looking at him seriously.

Drew swallowed then. "We're thicker than water, Summer." His eyes roamed my face, and he looked at me tenderly. "We will always be a part of each other's lives."

"I know," I smiled into his eyes. The look he gave me then, made me want to cup his cheek and kiss him. But I turned my head.

Drew cleared his throat. "So, Summer, I'm glad you're doing well. I see you're happier now.

With Nat. Is that what he wanted to hear? Was Drew fishing to see if he'd made the right decision walking away from me so Nat can be with me?

"Yes, I am," I said. "You made a very important decision for me, Drew, by walking away, by staying away from me." I couldn't help myself. I haven't seen him for so long, and now he was right next to me, finally giving me a chance to talk to him.

Drew's eyes darted to the front of class. Dr. Standish had walked up to the podium, dressed in his characteristically chic all black outfit. All eyes were trained on him. "Summer," Drew said. "I can't discuss this with you now. I have to get back to my seat."

"You came all the way up here to ask me how my arm was doing?" I asked. "Or to see if I was happy with Nat? What do you think, Drew?"

Drew had gotten up and was about to make his way back to the front of the classroom when he turned toward me, sprang up the steps back to where I was sitting, grabbed me from my seat, and pulled me out of the class until we were outside in the cool morning air, standing against the wall of the auditorium building. His blue eyes blazed into mine with such anger, desire, and frustration; I thought he was going to punch a hole into the wall and then take me against it.

"Dammit, Summer," Drew said, pushing me against the wall with his hard body. "Don't push it."

"I don't know what you're talking about," I said, looking into his eyes with pure innocence. "I wasn't part of the conversation you had with Nat about me."

"I didn't want to hurt you, disappoint you, Summer," Drew said. "Last summer when my mom was going through her divorce, and Dad was fooling around, everything seemed so bleak in our family. Then you were there, with your sweet beauty and sassy independence, your heart of gold, and innocence; you made everything better.

You made me want to be a better man." Drew's eyes searched my face, and my breath caught in my throat. "I wanted to be your hero, Summer. I wanted to see you look at me with that utter lost love that you always reserved for Nat."

"Drew…" I reached out my hand to touch his cheek. "You are my hero," I said. "If it wasn't for you showing up at the theater right then, I don't know if I would be here talking with you…"

Drew stepped close to me, encasing me against the wall and his body, a muscular arm holding me in place on both sides of me. He didn't touch me, but I can feel his skin heat up near mine. He didn't say anything, either, but from the way his eyes ate me up, anything he was thinking of saying would come out sounding too seductive for both of our ears. Drew had already made it clear he wanted me only in his friend zone. But the way both of us were staring at each other, it was going to be a struggle.

Finally Drew reached out a finger that went up to my face and gently tucked in a strand of hair that fell forward.

"We're missing class," I said.

"We can make it up," Drew said, unable to break our stare.

"Drew," I began, "I'm sorry for ever hurting you."

The words were out before I could take it back.

Then the switch. It took me completely by surprise. Drew's eyes went from adoration to indifference immediately as though he was another person, another personality.

"You didn't, Summer," he said blandly. "You couldn't hurt my feelings, especially when I didn't have strong ones to begin with, for you." He dropped his arms down, and stepped back, away from me.

I felt like someone had pulled the rug from underneath me.

Didn't have strong ones to begin with?

Did I imagine all the times Drew said he loved me?

"Well, if that's the case," I said. "I'm glad I know now how you really feel about me, Drew. It makes me feel a lot less guilty being with Nat, knowing you didn't really care for me as I thought."

Drew barely blinked as he coolly observed me. "You should go back to Nat," he said. "What we had…it was just a childhood crush. A stupid fantasy crush. Now that I'm grown up and in college, I realized that's all it was. I'm over it now and moving on. Dad was right. Why settle for one girl when you can have your pick in college."

"Drew…" I swallowed my tears. I wasn't going to let him see how much his words had hurt me. I should've known Drew wasn't sincere about how he felt about me this entire time. He was a player. He was unbelievably gorgeous. He knew the effect he had on women. He enjoyed sex way too much to wait it out for a girl like me., an innocent. He played me so well, got me to go to bed with him, take me as a conquest, and I never saw it coming… "Who are you?" I asked bitterly.

I raised my hand high in the air and let it fly as hard as it could across Drew's face. You could hear the smack clear across campus.

Drew nearly stumbled to the ground with the force of my slap. My volleyball arm could be a lethal weapon if I wanted to. I wanted to, briefly, but held back. Despite being as hurt and betrayed as I felt, deep down inside, I still saw the sweet beautiful boy, who tagged along with Rachel and me at Aunt Sookie's. I saw the young man, whose world was torn when his mother tried to commit suicide on fourth of July. Dammit, I still saw the Drew I had fallen half in love with.

I couldn't breathe. I couldn't believe this was happening. I rushed past Drew and ran to my seat to pick up my bag.

Trish took a good look at me, and handed me a piece of paper with her number on it. "You can borrow my notes. Call me."

"Thanks," I said, rushing out of the classroom before I could spot Drew coming in. I hurried to my car and fumbled to open the door. When I got in and locked all the doors, I felt the tremors go through me like tidal waves of sorrow. I kept crying, letting it all out.

All this time I feared I would break Drew's heart one day if Nat ever returned my love and we ended up together, but it was the opposite. Drew was the one who broke my heart, shattering the rock I thought he was for me. A betrayal like this hurt more than anything the haters and trolls tried to say or do against Aunt Sookie and me. It cut to the core, and I wasn't sure if I could ever forgive Drew.

Chapter 9

Nat arrived at the Pad earlier than usual. He was dressed up in a tie and suit as he walked through the door, which I had eagerly opened. Although he had a key of his own, having grown up at the Pad, I opened the door for him, I couldn't wait to see him.

As soon as he entered, I jumped him, wrapping my legs around his waist, as he crashed into me, up against the walls in the hallway, frantically kissing each other.

When my legs touched ground, I unbuttoned his suit jacket, took it off, and unbuttoned every button of his linen white shirt. He still wore a tie, which I loosen but left hanging around his neck. With the last button of his shirt undone, I took it off, and placed it on a chair, along with the suit jacket.

I kissed his bare muscular chest and stepped back, admiring his fit physique. He was hot. Wearing nothing but a tie and pants that was unbuttoned and ready to be slid right off, Nat looked like a sexy billionaire bad boy whose favorite activities were spent in the bedroom rather than the boardroom.

"Um, Summer," Nat grinned. "What's gotten into you?"

I kissed him hard, and he responded by grabbing my hair, fisting it, and bringing me closer to him. I finally broke off for air, and said, "Seeing you semi-dressed in a suit is so hot, Nat." As if demonstrating, I took hold of his tie and used it to pull him to me. We tangled for a while, undressing each other until we were making love on the sofa and then in the showers.

Sated and completely exhausted, we finally fell asleep together in each other's arms and woke up the next morning starting all over.

Nat finally got up and made breakfast for us. While he was cooking at the stove, I walked up to him and slipped my arms around his waist, and kissed him.

"What was that for?" Nat asked. "What did I do to deserve all this hot loving last night and this morning?" He was smiling, but there was a glint in his eyes, as though he knew there was something more.

"I realized how much I love you," I said.

"Great," Nat said, turning around to hug me. "Because I feel the same way about you."

"Good, then you wouldn't mind helping me at the Academy today," I said.

"Well, it's the first day of Spring classes, and I had scheduled two classes at the same time, thinking we would get that many students. The good news was that we did get that many students signed up, but the bad news is…there's only me teaching today."

"Who else was supposed to be teaching?" Nat asked.

"Of course not Rachel since she isn't here…"

"So that leaves… Drew?" Nat asked.

"Yes, but I haven't heard from him since yesterday," I said.

I winced at the painful memory of what happened between Drew and me.

Nat brought out his phone and began dialing. "Hey, Bro," he said. "Get your sorry lazy ass over here this morning."

Nat looked over at me and indicated he had Drew on the phone.

"Your face is bruised? So…what does that have to do with your ability to teach one of the improv classes today?" Nat started plating the spinach, turkey, and cheese omelet he made for me, adding some fresh diced tomatoes on top. He placed it in front of me, while still talking on the phone.

"Yes, Summer's here. Why wouldn't she be here?" Nat said. "You will see her at the Academy. She's teaching the other class." Nat looked angry then and said, "Look, Drew, I don't care how hung-over you are, you promised."

Nat finished his call to Drew right when I finished gobbling up the delicious breakfast he made.

"Hungry much?" Nat asked.

I laughed. "Always for anything Nat-made."

He plated his dish and came over to sit by me at the counter. "That's why I like cooking here at Aunt Sookie's...it feels appreciated."

"Well, I appreciate you, Nat," I said, squeezing his hand and looking into his beautiful sea green eyes.

Nat dropped his fork on the plate and leaned over to take my face in his hands before kissing me passionately until my toes curl. "Summer," he said, "the fact that you're with me, the fact I get to kiss you, hold you, and wake up next you in the morning; I consider myself the luckiest guy in the world. For that and everything else, especially you being in my life, I'm most appreciative."

I got up and hugged him, kissing the top of his head. "Well, Mr. Appreciative, I'm going to go take a quick shower, get dressed, and be ready for go. Oh, before I forget, remind me to bring that tray of fruit. We're having an open house kind of day. If you can look in the garage, I have a few party decorations I wanted to use for the celebration."

Nat was already gulping down his breakfast. "Go on, go take your shower, and I'll get the open house stuff ready to go."

I headed into the cozy bathroom shared by Rachel, me, and the boy, and started the shower. I undressed and stepped in, feeling instantly relaxed as the hot water poured down me from the large oversized showerhead. My arm was healing nicely, and I no longer needed a sling.

But it still made getting certain things like shampoo and soap harder.

I had lathered up my upper body, but couldn't reach the back scrubber on the top shelf. "Could you help me?" I called out to Nat. Then I lathered up my hair, washing my hair from roots to ends. I had closed my eyes while rinsing my hair, tilting my head back, enjoying the warmth of the water before I reached for the towel on the countertop near me. I wiped my face, patting it dry with the fluffy towel, and opened my eyes.

Kailin Gow

The room had steamed up, but it was still clear enough to see objects around, like some baskets filled with seashell soaps, lavender lotion, and fluffy white towels. How I loved the way Aunt Sookie had decorated the Pad to look like a Nantucket cottage.

I drew the curtains back, stepped out, and bumped into something…or someone really hard that I almost fell backwards.

I felt myself starting to panic, remembering how violated when I first saw all those private photos that crazy Sloane stalker took of me and Aunt Sookie,.

"Don't hurt me," I said. "Just leave me alone."

Strong arms enveloped me, and pulled me closer to him.

I started struggling to get out of his hold, but he held on, saying, "Shush, relax. I'm not going to hurt you."

I recognized that voice, and instantly felt more relieved.

Perfect Summer (Loving Summer #2)

When I got close enough to him, where he held me tight, stroking my back to comfort me, I looked up into the most beautiful blue eyes...eyes that belonged to Drew.

Drew was holding me in his arms like I was a precious child, stroking my back, and kissing the top of my head. "Shush, Summer," he said. "It's me, Drew. Not anyone else."

"Drew?" I asked, my mental cloud de-fogging along with the steam. The steam in the room made his hair unruly and wilder, and there was a purple bruise where I had slapped him at his cheekbone. He looked dangerously sexy with a growth of stubble.

"I heard you called for help, and I walked in, Summer." He stared down at me, and continued staring at my completely naked body standing less than an arm's length away from him. He was ogling, but I didn't care for some reason.

He'd seen, touched, and tasted me before, bringing me to multiple Drewgasms that one time I wanted to try casual sex, and he insisted it would be with him, if anyone.

After having such an intimate orgasmic experience like that with Drew, standing naked in front of him, felt so ordinary.

Without bothering to get dressed, knowing how Drew was watching me like a tiger ready to pounce on his prey, I walked over to the counter, picked up one of the starfish from the shelf, and traced it along the edge of my breasts.

Drew's eyes opened wider, and I saw him noticeably shuffled his feet, his tight jeans looking a little tighter.

I took a tube of body lotion, and squeezed the jasmine scented cream out onto my palm, and began spreading it over the skin of my stomach, my breasts, my legs, and my butt. I was going to put lotion on my back, but my arm wouldn't allow me to reach there.

"Let me help," Drew said, his voice barely a croak. He poured a large glob of lotion into his palms, and placed his hands on my shoulders and moved down, rubbing the lotion in as he firmly massaged and stroke his hands down my back, my hips, and the curve of my butt.

He was about to make his way down my butt and legs, when I heard the door slammed, and Nat's voice in the foyer. "Still taking a shower?" Nat called out. "I had to run out to pick up more food for Open House, and some party items. But Summer, we have to get going or we won't have time to set up, and we're still meeting Drew there. Or maybe here."

Drew looked at me and gestured for me to close the bathroom door.

I did and locked it, preventing any surprise visit from Nat.

Drew pulled me close to him again so that his lips were inches from my ear. "Let's not let Nat know about this," he said. "We didn't have sex, although I definitely wanted to."

When he said that, I could feel his arousal pressed against my lower back. I drew in a breath, smelling his cool fresh masculine scent, and let out a breath.

"Careful," I said, "one false move can start something big…something we wouldn't want."

Drew pressed up against me deliberately and grinded against my naked bottom with his jeans-clad erection. He sucked in some air, and said, "You don't realize how incredibly sexy you are, Summer. I can't stop staring at you and wanting to fuck you." He traced his fingers against my chin and jawline before he abruptly pushed me gently away from him. "Get dressed, and go with Nat to the Academy. I'll meet you there once the coast is clear."

Before I could say anything, Drew stepped as far away from me and went to the corner where he stood, hungrily watching me get dressed. His eyes never left mine, as I got dressed in record time.

I walked out of the bathroom, just wearing a black lace bra, a nude thong, and nice designer skinny jeans that hugged every curve like a second skin.

Nat was on the phone talking to someone from Donovan Dynamics when I came out and was headed to my room to grab a colorful blouse. He followed me to my room, finished his call, placed the phone on top of my dresser, and walked over to me.

"Had I known how hot you'd look just wearing a black bra with jeans, I wouldn't bother ever getting you lingerie. This..." he gestured at my outfit, "is the sexiest thing I've seen you wear." He bent his head down to nuzzle my collarbone, while his hands roamed over my exposed skin.

He unbuttoned my jeans and slipped his hand inside the front until his fingers were caressing my sensitive core. Before I could moan, his mouth crashed onto mine, swallowing my moan while his tongue plunged deeper into my mouth.

I was writhing against him, feeling the crest of a climax forming within me, when I noticed Drew standing at the doorway to my bedroom. It was like déjà vu, twice in a row, that Drew walked in when Nat and I were together. The first time he saw us, I was wracked with guilt and shame, but this time...since he said he didn't care about me that way and have no feelings towards me, I was turned on.

Apparently, he was too, as the large bulge in his jeans clearly showed.

His eyes met mine right when Nat pushed aside my bra and took one of my breasts into his mouth, causing me to arch my back, throwing my head back in passion. Nat's skilled fingers continued to plunge into me from below, and between his onslaught on my breast and his touch below, I started trembling with such intense pleasure, I cried out with the release, pulling Nat closer to me, scratching his back with my fingers.

When I opened my eyes and looked in the doorway, Drew was gone.

Nat looked up at me from where he was pushing my bra back over my breasts, and said, "I know we're running late now...but it was worth it, wasn't it?" He pulled his hand out of my jeans, and buttoned the top. "There," he smiled. "Good as new. Now let's put a top on you before I do a repeat performance on you, and skip today's classes at the Academy altogether."

Perfect Summer (Loving Summer #2)

"Nat!" I pushed him away. "We have to be at there for the Open House." I went to my closet, pulled out a green blouse with flowing sleeves and a self-belt, slipped it on, and went to the mirror to brush my hair. I put on small gold earrings, then took out a wand of lipgloss, dabbed at my lips, puckered, and wiped. With just a touch of violet eyeliner which brought out my green eyes, and mascara, I was ready to go.

"Wow," Nat said, gathering me for a kiss. "You're the only girl I know who can get ready in less than five minutes, and look like you just walked out of Cosmopolitan magazine."

I smiled. "Well, you know me, Nat, I'm really a tomboy at heart. I have no patience for any beauty routine that will take more than an hour."

Nat grinned, "That's my Summer. No wonder all the boys liked you. You were one of us, but then..." he cupped my breasts, "you grew these glorious breasts, developed soft beautiful curves, had soft touchable flawless skin, and an attitude that makes men just want more from you." Nat pulled me in for a kiss, and said, "Knowing how much of an effect you have on guys, Summer, I probably have to get used to the fact that I'm with one of the most desirable women in town, that men would throw themselves at you. Because if I ever saw you with another man, unless I can get it under control…this crazy jealousy, I have to admit, I'd be insanely jealous."

"Nat…" I smiled, wanting to change the subject…did he see Drew here? "Same goes for you. I'd be insanely jealous seeing you with someone else, too." I looked at the clock in the living room, and gasped. "Got to go now, Nat! We only have ten minutes. Quick, grab all the food. I'll get the bags of party favors."

In record time, we had my SUV loaded with food and party decorations with Nat in the passenger seat while I took all the shortcuts to the Academy.

The parking lot was full when I pulled up to my reserved parking. The doors to the Academy were already open, and students ranging in age from seven to fourteen were walking in with their parents.

Perfect Summer (Loving Summer #2)

Nat and I grabbed everything we could and headed into the Academy from the back entrance, usually reserved for the theater crew when the Academy used to be a working local theater. From there, we placed everything in the kitchen, where there seemed to be a large display of catered foods – a cheese and ham spread, fruits, raw vegetables, stuffed mushrooms, fried dumplings, and meatballs.

A girl with blonde hair in a ponytail, dressed in all black and wearing a black apron came in with a silver tray, which she filled up with more food.

Another girl with red hair came in and did the same thing.

Nat and I looked at each other before I asked, "Who ordered catered services?"

The pretty blonde girl said, "Oh, we're from the studios," she said, handing me a card. Lisa. "We normally cater events like film releases, but this was very last minute and smaller."

"From the studios?" I asked. Where was I going to have a budget to afford this for a small acting school like ours?

"Yes, the one Astor Fairway had contracted for his next film. Cold Desert Studios."

"So Astor Fairway hired you to be here?" I asked.

"Well, it was a friend of his who got a hold of us, told us the contract was ours for the rest of the year for film releases if we can make this one work, last minute. We only had an hour to get this all done, believe it or not. Luckily, our restaurant is a couple of blocks away, and we had all this ready to go. Just needed heating up."

"It wasn't Astor who hired you?" I asked. "Then who?"

"I did," a familiar male voice came from the doorway. I looked up into the ceiling, unable to believe that it was Drew who arranged all this.

"Drew?" Nat said, incredulously. "How did you figure we'd probably need something like this?"

Perfect Summer (Loving Summer #2)

Drew's eyes burned into mine, the intensity of his desire for me clearly on his face. The memory of his hands rubbing lotion on my body, and then the heated hunger in his eyes as he watched me with Nat; made my face flushed with desire. I looked down, not wanting to betray how I felt, in front of Nat and the caterers.

Drew's eyes didn't falter from looking at me. "When you called me to remind me of my promise to help out at the Academy and told me I had to be here today for the Open House and class, I went ahead and arranged all this…thanks to the help of Astor, who seemed to know a lot of people in town."

I couldn't help smiling to myself, a little surprised but happy with how well Astor had started getting along with the boys…now that he no longer dated me.

"Well, good thinking, Drew," I said, walking up to him and patting him on the shoulder. "This…is incredible!"

Drew's gaze drank me in from head to toe. "It's the least I could do, Summer." He winced as he tried to smile.

I reached out to touch his bruised cheek, and instantly felt horrible. "I'm sorry I slapped you," I said. "I should never have resort to that. It's not in my nature to be violent."

Drew looked pained and said softly, "I probably had it coming, Summer." He laughed. "Not the slap, but the anger."

"I don't even want to revisit why I felt the anger, Drew, not right now or I'd lose it. I'm still not quite over everything you said to me."

"Summer," Drew's eyes looked so sad at the moment. "I wished I can take back what I said. "But it's already out there, and this is a way to make it back to you."

"Drew…"

"So, how's the food?" another familiar voice said from the doorway.

I turned and saw Astor standing there, his arms crossed casually around his chest. He was wearing a USC t-shirt and loose black jeans that fell down to black combat boots.

The two caterers looked from Astor, Drew, and Nat to me, and exchanged looks. "Some people get all the luck," one of them muttered as they headed out with their trays stacked high with food.

I rushed over to Astor and hugged him, welcoming him into the kitchen where he immediately headed to the table for some food. "Is the food alright?" he asked again.

"Haven't tried it," I said. I took one of the stuffed mushrooms and popped it into my mouth. It was good, decent as you would expect it to be, but not earth-shattering good. "What do you think?" I popped one of the mushrooms into Astor's mouth while Drew and Nat busied themselves with sampling some of the food, too.

"Ehh, it's alright," Astor said.

"I know," I smiled over at Drew and Nat, who were standing next to each other, watching me joke with Astor, taking samples of the food. "This is good, though. I wouldn't be able to get this all together on such short notice so this is all good."

Astor smiled at me, his eyes crinkling with such affection. "I wanted to do something special for you, Summer, especially with the attack here and all. Thank goodness, there's a restraining order against Sloane for getting anywhere remotely close to you."

"Thank you for getting all that done for me...the police report, getting the office cleaned up..."

"I had help, Summer. Your friends there happened to be well connected in certain circles, and they helped to get things going faster than normal." He stepped aside and walked over to Nat and Drew, who were talking.

"Hey, thanks for all your help with the Sloane incident," Astor said. "Donovan Dynamics really does know its stuff."

Nat glanced at me and said, "No problem, we were actually already working on Summer's case so we had a head start in resources and research."

"Cool," Astor said. "I went to the right security firm then." Astor turned to Drew and said, "What do you think of the catering? Does it live up to your standards?"

"They're fine," Drew said. "Good recommendation, Fairway, considering there isn't much of a choice when you only have an hour to get caterers at the last minute like this."

"That or you and Nat could have whipped up something and brought it over," I said. "Your cooking is wonderful. I bet you could've made something better than this in an hour."

Nat grinned, "But Summer, we didn't have an hour at the time. You were busy showering and getting ready, while I had to go out to buy food, and…" Nat went over to the food we brought in. "Forgot about this," he said. He took the food out of the containers and arranged them on the caterers' trays before heading out to the main floor of the Academy.

Astor looked over at Drew. "Summer usually doesn't take more than an hour to get ready, and she takes the fastest showers, guess this Open House is a big deal for her."

At the word "shower", I noticed Drew glanced quickly at me, before looking away. I blushed and also looked away…thinking about my heated shower incident with Drew.

Drew looked down at the ground for a second, before he said, "Hey, talking about the Open House, someone has to be out there talking up a storm to get people to enroll." He came over to me, kissed me on the cheeks, and walked out.

Astor came over and sat next to me. "Finally, alone! I just spent twenty minutes talking to people, but most of them just wanted me to sign things and take pictures with them. I figured, my area of expertise is to actually get some of them to sit in the sample class we have later, and get them involved in the acting."

"Good idea," I said.

"I have another idea that I've been thinking about for a while. I wanted to tell you what it was that night you were attacked, but forgot. Some things were more important at the time…and that's you." Astor hesitated and said, "I worry about you, Summer. Not just that Aunt Sookie's not here, but that you have these haters and stalkers willing to go to fanatic extremes to hurt you or mess with you. And you're taking on so much with this school and college. Believe me, I know how it feels to have the pressure to keep taking on more things and more, thinking it would help your career; but after a while it takes its toll, and you burn out. I don't want to see that happening with you."

Astor took my hand and played with my fingers. "I want you to be taken care of, to be cared for." Astor entwined his hand in mine and brought it to his lips, kissing my knuckles. "I want to do this for you...for Aunt Sookie's memory. I want to become a partner with you at the Academy, maybe buy a part of it so at least you can get funding. Plus, it'll probably stop some of the haters hired by your rival schools from attacking the school and you."

Astor kissed my hand again, and sat closer to me. "We can hire some of the best acting coaches to teach here once in a while. We can offer more classes. It's something I'd love to do with you, Summer." He turned to me and brushed a strand of hair off my face. "This will give me some stability, and it'll be something I'd like to be part of like that digital library. When I'm finished with this next film, I'm taking a few months off to take film classes at

USC." He smiled happily. "I get to stay here and finally get into something normal, but best of all…" he looked deeply into my eyes. "I can have that chance to have a normal relationship."

I was speechless. This was so unexpected. "Astor, I'd love for you to get involved with the Academy. You're always welcome to, but Aunt Sookie left this Academy for me and the Donovans to run. I'll have to ask them what they think. But I'm so happy you're not going to be traveling so much to locations. You'll get to be here…"

Astor grinned happily. "I know. I get to go to the same school as you, maybe even take the same classes, and be here for you when you need me, not out in some camp filming the next blockbuster film that takes place in the woods."

I laughed. "Some of the best films take place in the woods."

"I know…" Astor said.

"Hey," Nat came in and looked at Astor and me sitting so closely together. He stopped, and a look of jealousy crossed his face briefly as he saw Astor drop my hand. He came up to me and put his arm around me. "There were a lot of people asking about upcoming classes and the schedule for summer, too, beside the spring ones. I know you mentioned you were working on setting up the summer school schedule, but do we have copies of them to give people?"

"That's exactly what I was trying to work on, but, have been, um, distracted these past weekends, to actually spend time on it." I coughed. Nat should know. He had been spending every weekend with me, making love to me, and making me forget all about my duties and obligations.

Nat shot me a heated look, clearly replaying some of the heated weekends we've spent together, in his mind. "That's okay, Summer, I'll just tell everyone the schedule is being finalized, and it will be up in on the website when it's ready."

"Good!" I said. "I'll work on it this week."

"I'll keep out of your hair for a while, Summer," Nat said. "So you can get it finished...then afterwards..."

he gave me a wicked smile that sent a heated sensation through me.

Astor's face was expressionless as he watched Nat walk out the door. He bent to finger the charm bracelet Nat had given me, that I was wearing. "Nice bracelet," Astor said. "Looks like Nat has the same taste in jewelers as I do."

I blushed, knowing that Astor was trying to play it cool, but wasn't really cool about it. But he was here, and he had catered the Open House with Drew, and was about to teach a class just because…he liked me still? Even after we broke up twice, publicly?

"Astor," I said gently. "I really enjoy being with you and I love everything you stand for and have a passion for, but I don't want to give you any mixed messages, lead you on or anything like that. But I'm getting pretty serious with Nat."

Astor's face fell then, and he said, "I kinda felt that vibe in here just now." He paused, "Although I always thought you and Drew…there was something there, too."

"Astor," I took his hand in both of my hands. "I'll always be your friend though. I think that's probably more of a lasting relationship than anything anyways, and…"

"I know, I know…" Astor said, embarrassed. "We both don't know what the future holds, of course. I just shouldn't have come on so strong. Anyways, let's get moving. We have some classes to teach!"

"Ready when you are," I said, walking out of the kitchen with him.

Chapter 10

Nat

Open House turned out to be a bigger success than we had imagined, with several of the students enrolling for spring classes and signing up for the waiting list for summer classes. Not only was it a fun event for Summer and the students enrolling, but it gave me an opportunity to talk to Astor, who had now become part of our team at Donovan Dynamics working on trying to provide Summer with more security as well as find out more about the haters and Sloane who had physically attacked Summer.

As much as I disliked the guy in the beginning, thought he was some kind of spoiled overindulgent wuss pretty boy actor, Astor Fairway actually impressed me with a brilliant plan. He was going to have a press conference that day at the Open House, where he would make a dramatic announcement to the press and his public. The press and paparazzi came out to the Academy in droves, hoping to find out more about the top secret film project he was working on as an actor and possibly as a producer. Astor was planning on talking a little about his upcoming film, which his fans wanted to know all about. A film he actually read the book series for, while on plane rides flying back and forth between home and location shoots.

The theater and classrooms were jammed packed later that afternoon as the press filed in with their large cameras and equipment. Word got out that Astor Fairway was teaching a special class at the school, and was planning on teaching there permanently when he finished filming his latest film, Fade.

Having high hopes for Fade, as a career-making acting role for him, Astor told the press, he was hoping to take some time after filming to go back to school to be a filmmaker, yet still be in touch with the public by teaching classes at Aunt Sookie's Acting Academy.

Fade, a dystopian young adult film set in a future Nevada desert was based on a bestselling young adult book series. Astor was to play the leading man, Jack Simple, a sophisticated James Bond-like hero, who was assigned to protect a mysterious beautiful young woman named Celestra Caine. Celestra appeared to be a normal high school senior who was involved in track, had a boyfriend who adored her, and a typical family in the suburbs of Virginia. Little did she know, when she returned from school after track practice one day, the world that she knew, was about to change dramatically, and everything she thought was real turned out to be something else entirely. What did she know, and who was Celestra? Why were the government's top secret agency after her, and why was there a strong connection between her and Jack Simple?

There wasn't much in the press about Astor's latest film since the producers wanted to keep spoilers from leaking. But there were buzz from the fans of the series that helped put the project in front of Astor and his agent.

"It's the role of a lifetime!" Astor's agent told him, although the film didn't have a major studio attached to it yet. The role of Jack Simple was complex enough to challenge any young actor's acting talents, yet sexy enough to still bring out the sex appeal of the leading actor. Jack Simple was a man's man and a true cool badass, while also being a ladies' man. Astor liked that the script was actually written by the series' author, which would appeal and appease the fans of the book series. When he first read the script, he enjoyed the appeal to all audience members – men would love the rapid-fire action, women would love the swoon-worthy romance and hot love triangle between Jack Simple and Celestra, and Celestra and her ex-boyfriend Greyson.

The storyline was huge and dramatic, and complex enough to appeal to a wide audience, and with four books in the series, Fade would be ideal to adapt into a franchise. It was the first film Astor was actually excited about acting in since he could appreciate the storyline and thought the positive message about love and life, was something worth telling through film.

"I'll finance part of it if I have to," Astor said to the media. "It's a great story with a compelling plot. I would love to be a producer for this film. It's going to be hot."

Was there funding?

"A private equity and a group of investors had stepped in to fund the film. It's got great international range, too, and I think international distributors were already being secured."

Afterwards, when everyone left, I went up to Astor and thanked him.

"What for?" Astor asked.

"For using your fame and influence for a good cause. That was quick-thinking getting the press here for your conference to talk about upcoming films and plans. I'm sure that extra would help Summer and this school out."

"Well, that's the goal," Astor said. "I think that's everyone's goal, anyone who cared for Summer...to help and support her in every way."

I nodded in agreement. "You know, Astor, you're not that bad, after all."

"You should know, I'm now one of your clients at Donovan Dynamics."

"Right, and that extra security you asked for Summer, we were already planning that. Plain-clothes men still looked suspicious on campus, especially if they're in their late 30s, which most of our security staff were. We've started hiring college-aged looking security, but they're going to take some time to train. Right now, Astor, we have to count on Drew being there on campus with Summer. He had already taken it upon himself to watch her, but he'd been going through some issues of his own, which would make it hard for him to be with her all the time."

"As long as Summer has someone there," Astor said.

"Don't worry, Drew won't let anything happen to Summer," Nat said. "He'd probably give his own life for her."

"All of us would," Astor said drily. "Between all of us watching out for her, Sloane and his group of sick perverts won't be able to find her alone like he did that night."

"He is a sick fuck, isn't he?" I said. "First his obsession with Aunt Sookie, and now with Summer. It's a crying shame our justice system allowed a sicko who attacked girls and mess with their minds like that can be left walking freely, capable and free to do it again or to another girl. Sorry there wasn't enough for them to lock up Sloane, this time. But we're still working on it. The asshole is smarter than he looks. We suspect he may be connected to something bigger than being a stalker, but all the evidence we've found had been tampered with so it's taking a while for our team to find something on him."

"As long as they're working on it," Astor said seriously. "Well, the good news for Summer is that I'll be taking some classes, auditing them at USC so if Drew can't be there for her with his issues, at least I can."

I gave him a dry smile. Good news for him and Summer, of course, but I also knew the golden boy wasn't over his feelings for Summer. I should be glad Summer had so many devoted guy friends, but it also made me jealous as hell, because I knew what those guy friends wanted from her, and it wasn't just being friends.

I was jealous about Drew being on campus with Summer, but had to live with it since she needed all the protection she could get. And I couldn't personally be there to protect her. While she and I had grown closer since I finally allowed myself to be with her (the dumbest mistake I've ever made was to push her away all those years!), we still weren't officially committed as a couple.

But I wanted to be…and we were getting there, with my weekends spent with her, and every single chance I could get to fly out to Malibu, I took it. I was committed to making this long distance relationship between Summer and I work.

And as far as I knew, Summer was, too…but it seemed every time Drew was around, there was this chemistry between them that I couldn't even deny. It was what made them such good friends growing up, and now that they were grown up, there certainly was this attraction they had.

I wasn't going to push the issue. I wanted to give the chance I have with Summer my all. And I did, especially when it came to making love to her.

That part came all too easily. It was like a dam burst of passion between us. Like we've been holding back all this pent up emotions and sexual wants between us for years, and it finally came out. Every time it got better and better. Now one look at her or even a slight touch from her can give me a massive hard-on…like my body can't react otherwise when I'm near her or in her presence.

I could tell she felt the same way. The body doesn't lie. Her response to my kisses, her moans and the pleasure she took in my touch, told me she enjoyed it as much as I did. Her nipples are always already hard when I take off her bra and begin licking them, and by the time I stick my fingers into her, she'd be wet and ready for me.

I haven't seen any of that kind of chemistry between her and Astor. I had him beat there. But Drew...he had that natural charm and appeal women could not get enough of. I know it worked on Summer, but because of her devotion to her lifelong crush on me (thank God!), she held back.

I don't know. Maybe she did love me more than Drew or thought I would be better for her but all I knew was that this was that I was having the best time of my life being with her. The happiness she brought me being with her was something I couldn't even thought possible. I loved her so much more than ever.

But I was also aware that Drew was there and would always be there between us. Even when he told me he was backing down to let me have my chance with Summer again so he could move on and start dating other girls, even when he told Summer that he no longer cared for her that way; again the body doesn't lie. He still wants her.

The question I have and that I was more concerned about was: how much did Summer want him?

Chapter 11

Summer

I was on cloud nine the rest of the week, thinking of how well the Open House went, and how the boys, including Astor got along so well at the event. It made me think that maybe one day when I finally did settle down with one of them or maybe someone else entirely, they would be fine with it, that they would not go crazy and do something stupid. We were all, somehow or another, brought together by fate. Or the karma of Aunt Sookie. To see everyone getting along and not fighting, was the most amazing and heartwarming feeling for me since I cared for all of them so much.

Although I was on a high, getting Nat to me all weekend long, and continuing on with his passionate lovemaking; I was happier knowing that Drew did have feelings for me. It was clear as day, the way he looked at me throughout the Open House, and the way he tried to find an opportunity to brush against me or to touch me.

Then why did he tell me that he never had any feelings for me, that they were never strong? Why did he acted like I was just another one of his sexual conquests and that our relationship meant nothing more than a night of casual sex?

He said he was over me, that he realized what he felt for me was just a childhood fantasy. He was over it, and it was time he grew up, start sampling more of the offerings readily available to him on campus.

Was that how he felt? Did he truly just act like he cared about me, just to fulfill his lustful needs?

The Drew I saw at the Open House, the Drew that surprised me in the showers, was the one I thought I knew.

Then seeing him again with those girls in front of the class during Classical Literature and Drama, brought all the sense of insecurity and jealousy back. They were all over him, touching him, whispering in his ears, and even massaging his neck and back.

Drew was relishing the attention, the sex god with his harem of pretty and easily available girls.

One of the girls kissed him fully on the mouth, and proceeded to inch her way almost onto his lap.

"Oh brother," I muttered. "Isn't that pure shameless?"

"What? Trying to fight over that football star?" Trish said, looking through her librarian-style glasses at Drew.

"It's so comical," I said. "They're practically elbowing each other out of the way to get his attention."

"Who is he?" Trish asked. "I mean, he looks like he's used to all that attention, like he's famous or something."

"He's Drew," I said. "We've known each other since toddlers. He got a scholarship to play football here at USC."

"No, besides that," Trish said. "I've seen him somewhere before…"

"San Francisco?"

"No, he's quite a hottie, isn't he? I bet he's been on television or have modeled before," Trish said, taking out her phone and typing in it.

"He's grown up better-looking than I expected," I said.

"Oh, there he is...Drew Donovan, from the Donovan Family, models the latest Dolce and Gabbana underwear at the Nob Hill Society Annual Charity."

I practically grabbed the phone out of her hands, and stared open-mouth at a photo of Drew all sweaty and gleaming, without a stitch of clothing on, except for a black tiny brief that barely covered his groin area. He was rippled, smooth-skinned, tanned, and incredibly hot. Those clear blue eyes looked dreamily into the camera, and his expression was blissfully tortured and heart-wrenching. Every woman who had a heartbeat would be hot for him. Every woman would want to soothe him, plunge their fingers into his thick wavy black hair and kiss away that pained expression in his eyes.

Perfect Summer (Loving Summer #2)

"Gulp," I said. This was another Drew I haven't really gotten to know. This God sent to women. Besides Nat, he was probably the most gorgeous male species on Earth. I swallowed. He was right about what he said to me...he did have his pick of girls, especially during college. Why should he care about me, wait for me to give into him?

I was feeling so insecure about Drew, yet now highly aroused by looking at his photo, I barely saw the text that flashed across my phone: "Hi – I'm here!" until I saw a familiar friendly face belonging to a crown of golden hair enter the room from one of the front side entrance. I smiled.

Astor Fairway had made it to class.

I waved to Astor where I was sitting and he waved back. He made his way to the front of the steps to go up to my seat in the back, but a bunch of girls (mostly from Drew's harem) flew up and surrounded him, demanding autographs and pictures.

It was like that time when Astor and I went to Disneyland and an entire crowd surrounded him, thanks to Drew.

Drew? I looked over to where he was sitting, and he was now alone. All the girls who had surrounded him were now crowded around Astor. Could he had put them up to it?

I was staring hard at Drew's back when he turned around and looked straight at me.

"He's even more gorgeous in person," Trish said drily next to me.

Was that a smile on his face?

Gorgeous or not, I put aside my insecurity, got up, and walked down to where Astor was... signing autographs and taking pictures with some of the girls.

Drew got up, too, walking towards me.

I shot daggers at him to stay where he was. He was not going to do this to poor Astor again.

"Excuse me," I barged through the crowd forcefully. "But the Professor wants everyone in their seats now or we can't start the class on time. Everyone back to your seats. And you..." I pointed at Astor, "Come with me."

Perfect Summer (Loving Summer #2)

I fisted Astor's t-shirt in front, and pulled him behind me headed up to my seat in the back row. I didn't realize how I looked holding onto his shirt, and pulling him behind me like he was a hot prisoner of mine, but when I heard whistles coming from the guys in class, I realized I probably look like some kind of BDSM dominatrix in some wild erotica film leading my lover to some playroom dungeon for wild unbridled sex. I glanced down. I was wearing short white cut-off jeans, a man's white wife beater tank top (must be Nat's), and my black lace bra underneath. My hair was down, a little messy and wild from trying to air dry it this morning because I was running late and had grabbed Nat's shirt to put on this morning.

I looked to my side and I looked down, it seemed all eyes were on Astor and me. Including Drew, who had that intense hungry look he gave me all weekend long. I smiled. If Drew wanted to put the sexy on, I can too.

I lifted my head higher, push out my chest, and walked confidently up the steps to my seat next to Trish and patted the empty one next to me for Astor.

Astor sat down and leaned in to whisper a quick "thanks" in my ear, which tickled me, causing me to laugh out loud.

That made Drew turn around to look at me again, his face clearly angry.

I leaned into Astor and whispered, "Of all the classes to audit, you had to choose this one."

Astor whispered back, "What's wrong with this one?"

"Nothing," I said. "Just that this is a very tough class. There's even a mandatory study group we have to take to make sure we understand the lecture, apparently."

Astor grinned. "Sounds like a challenge."

I smiled back, "It is."

Astor cozied up next to me, "Of course whether this class is tough or not, I have another reason to be here."

He reached for my hand, entwined his fingers through them, and raised it to his lips to kiss my fingertips.

Trish next to me, arched her eyebrows, and darted her eyes to the front of the room.

I followed in her direction, just in time to see Drew stomping up the steps toward us, his face trained towards me unrelentlessly.

"Summer," Drew said, looking at me intently as though he didn't even see Astor next to me, nor Trish to my left. "I need to talk to you."

"Class is about to start, Drew," I said. "I don't want to miss another week's class like last week."

"You can get notes, a bunch of the girls gave me theirs for last week's class. I can share them with you."

"Astor's auditing the class tonight," I said.

"It's urgent," Drew said. "I just need to talk to you for a few minutes, then we'll be back in class."

"Is that alright with you, Astor?" I asked.

Astor looked slightly annoyed. "As long as he's a gentleman to you."

I looked at Drew and said to Astor, "Drew is many things, but he's never been ungentlemanly."

"Good," Astor said, "Because I really want to enjoy this lecture tonight. A friend of mine is guest lecturing, and I don't want to miss it on account of someone being an a-hole to a good friend of mine." He looked from me to Drew.

Drew's jaw twitched then, and before he can say anything, I got up, took his hand, and led him out of the auditorium to where we were last week, outside in the morning air and against the walls of the school building.

"What do you want?" I asked, leaning against the wall and crossing my arms.

Drew's eyes narrowed at me, and he growled angrily at me. "Do you have to ask?" Before I could answer, Drew pushed me up against the wall with his body, until I was held suspended by him against the wall. "Do you have to make this so difficult for me? Torture me like this, make me so insane with jealousy, I can't even think straight. First Nat and now Astor. At least with Nat, I know where I stand, but Astor…you can't go back to him again just because he promised to remain here and not travel as much for his films."

"That's none of your business, Drew," I said.

"It *is* my business," he said. "It's my business to keep you safe, to watch over you, but I'm finding it harder and harder because all I want to do when I think of you is to get close to you, not stay away."

He brought his lips so close to mine, and hovered there for the longest time, as though torn.

"I promised myself I would stay away from you, emotionally and physically," Drew said.

He inched closer.

"I promised myself I wouldn't fall for you again once I shut down any feelings I have for you."

Closer still.

"I've tried and tried to stay away from you, to feign indifference, even surrounding myself with the hottest girls on campus, but I'm so fucked in love with you I'm beyond repair."

"Drew," I whispered. "I don't want you to be repaired."

"But I do, Summer," he said softly. "How am I going to be able to stand a whole lifetime of wanting my brother's girl and not be able to have her?"

"Drew," I bit my lips. "I'm not married to Nat. We're not even officially a couple, but we are close and getting closer. It's the truth, and I don't want to mislead you or hurt you in anyway." I patted his hand. "Astor is a very good friend. He wants more, too, but I don't know if what we have can sustain a lifetime of love."

"What about me?" Drew asked. "Would there, was there ever a chance for me?"

I looked down and bit my lips. "I don't know. That depends on you, Drew."

*****

Drew and I walked back to the classroom, taking our seats, right when the guest lecturer came in.

If I didn't have my hands full trying to sort out my feelings for three very hot and attractive men, I would have gone gaga over the strikingly handsome professor who strode in.

He was tall, muscular but lean, lightly tanned, had high cheekbones, a chiseled face, beautiful blue eyes, and wavy black hair. In his late twenties, and dressed like he walked out of a GQ magazine in black slacks and a silky black shirt.

The entire room fell silent as some of the more well-read students recognized who just walked into the room.

"Hi," he began, "I'm Professor Sebastian Sorensen, and I'm here today because your regular professor Dr. Standish had to give a lecture in England." He smiled, which showed dimples along with a cleft in his chin that made the girls in front give a collective sigh.

"What's with the parade of hot men today?" Trish muttered.

I smiled back at her. "Seems like they travel in packs."

Astor nudged me and whispered. "Sorensen is brilliant. He's won best musical composition at the Oscars, the Academy, and even Tony's. He's only in his late twenties, too, and have produced some amazing films and plays. *Rock Hard, Love Hard* was one he produced and wrote the music for. It was a hit in Vegas, and there were more..."

Astor sank back into his seat, and listened intently to every word Professor Sorensen was lecturing. I sank back into mine, relaxing into the fascinating lecture about music composition in dramatic plays and musicals.

For the next forty minutes, Professor Sorensen commanded the room masterfully, regaling the class with stories about some of his music, and stories about his Hollywood experiences working on the music side of filmmaking. He talked about his experience getting started, and how he first started his career as a choir boy in a boarding school in Europe, and how when he discovered music, it opened a world of new experiences and opportunities for him.

Time flew quickly, and finally the lecture concluded, earning the professor a standing ovation.

"Thank you for being such an attentive and inquisitive group," he said. "You'll have your delightful professor Standish back next week, but if you want to get ahold of me, you can follow me on Twitter at @BeMyProtege so everyone, this concludes the lecture, if you weren't sure." He smiled a charming little secret smile that had all the girls sighing.

Afterwards the swarm of girls in front swept into try to talk to the sexy professor, while I watch Drew's harem at it once again.

"You'd think these girls don't ever get any attention from guys, the way they're acting so desperately."

"More like they're looking for the best guy, while ignoring the guys they think aren't good enough for them," Trish said.

"So, first Drew, then Astor, and now darkly handsome Professor Sorensen," I said.

Trish looked seriously at me. "The crème of the crop. Not only handsome good looks, but wealthy and famous, as well."

I looked over at Astor, who had stood up, and had extended his hand to help me up. "Come meet Sorensen, Summer. You'll find him fascinating."

"Sure, but first…" I asked Trish if she's heard about the study group's first meeting yet. I had to attend and try to catch up on missing a couple of lectures already.

"I don't have the location where they will be at this week, but here's the url to their blog. They seem to post the time and location of the group's meeting last minute on there so check that out first for the next meeting."

"Thanks Trish," I said. "You've been so helpful…maybe we can catch a bite to eat for lunch after class next week or something."

Trish blushed and shrugged. "Sure, Summer. Thanks!"

Astor held my hand going down the steps to Sorensen who was still surrounded by the girls, some of them more bold than the other.

Sorensen was trying to be polite, as one girl after another, kept asking him personal questions instead of anything that related to his work.

I looked at Astor, and he nodded. It was Operation Save the Hottie time.

I got ready to barge through the crowd like I had with Astor, but found they weren't as easy to de-band as before.

I couldn't make my way through to Sorensen, the crowd was relentless in trying to get to talk to him, but I wasn't going to give up.

"Planning to launch a strike?" Astor asked.

"You could say that." I was about to head through the crowd again, when out came a large muscular body who literally plow through the crowd with his body to stand before Sorensen.

Sorensen saw Drew approach him, and smiled widely. "Hey Drew," Sorensen said. "Nice to see you're in college now." He looked around him. "Where's Nat?"

"He's in San Francisco," Drew said.

"I'll be visiting up north in a couple of days," Sorensen said. "I'll stop by the family home to say 'hi'"

"Mom'll love that," Drew said. "And so would Rachel."

"Then I'll book the flight tonight," Sorensen said. "I' may have to visit Donovan Dynamics for a customized security system. Had a break-in recently. Knew I shouldn't trust my mother's designer to handle my place's security."

"They'll know what to do," Drew said.

"I'm hoping so," Sorensen said.

Drew stepped to the side then when Sorensen spotted Astor.

"Hello Fairway," he said, "ready to shoot the new film?"

"Very," Astor said. "And I'm glad that the producers chose your song for the opening."

"Fade will be a spectacular production," Sorensen said. "I really got into the story and was glad I can use a bit of flair to compose the score for the rest of the film."

"Can't wait to see it," I said, beaming.

"Me too!" Sorensen cheerfully exclaimed, smiling a grin that was breathtaking. It sent a thrill through me, and I momentarily forgot I was already involved in a very complicated relationship. I shook my head.

I would have gone on with the questions and getting to know him better, when someone bumped me from behind, causing me to nearly fall forward into Sorensen. Astor caught me just in time, and used both arms to steady me.

A student in a non-descript grey sweatshirt, walking shorts, and a cap that covered most of his face muttered "sorry," but kept walking on.

I had dropped my bag when he bumped into me, and when I bent to pick it up, I saw a note beside it.

STUDY GROUP MEETING TONIGHT at 7 in the science building, lab 5.

I smiled. What a coincidence. I was about to go online to check the schedule, but now I didn't have to.

Chapter 12

The science building where the study group's meeting to be held was a bit too dark for my liking. It was 7 pm, and I still didn't see anyone else show up for the meeting, but I went ahead to the door of the building, hoping to see if it was unlocked.

I tried the door, and it gave way, opening up just enough for me to enter the building.

Except for some light at the end of the hallway, which seemed to be coming from one of the rooms, the hallway was dark, almost pitch black.

I pulled out my phone and quickly sent a text to Drew, wondering where he was. I thought he'd agreed to meet me for the meeting, if he could make it.

Perfect Summer (Loving Summer #2)

A text came back immediately from Drew.

DREW: I'M RUNNING LATE BECAUSE OF FOOTBALL PRACTICE, BUT I'LL BE THERE.

ME: GOOD. SEE YOU SOON. BUT I THINK EVERYONE ELSE IS LATE.

After I sent him the information where the classroom was, and which building, I put my phone away in my jeans pocket, and walked faster toward the room with the light. Maybe everyone was already inside, and I was lingering outside while they waited for stragglers to show up.

As I rounded the corner a couple of doors from the room, I heard a faint sound come from there…the cheesy music to an 80s show. It was oddly familiar, but not familiar enough where I can recognize it immediately.

I finally reached the room and was about to walk in when I noticed there was no one there. No other students, just a small computer monitor in the middle of the room, playing the music loudly while collages of photographs flashed across the screen.

The walls seemed to enclose me, as I recognized in horror the same collage made of my personal photos and of Aunt Sookie's were flashing on screen. The same one left on my computer at the Academy. Sloane's.

The music of the television show came clearly to me then. It was the theme song to The Red Phoenix, the only science fiction show Aunt Sookie had been in, playing the beautiful super heroine Red Phoenix.

It dawned on me what this was about...a set up. Whoever left me that note about the study class, had purposely gave me the wrong information, leading me here.

I was not going to panic. I hurriedly walked out of the room and began almost running down the hall. At first I thought I heard footsteps following me, but I kept going, towards the front door of the Science building, which was at the far end.

Thanks to my volleyball practices, I was still in top athletic shape, but the distance to the door seemed so far away. I was almost to the door when a dark figure jumped in front of me. He was big and tall, and from the shadows in the dark, he wore a baseball cap. The student in the grey sweatshirt who had bumped into me today.

Instantly my heartbeat rose, and my body responded to the familiar foul scent of the man, who had attacked me at Aunt Sookie's Academy by recoiling at first, and then getting ready to fight. The memory of him grinding on me as he broke my elbow and shoved his grubby hands into my mouth to keep me from screaming, made my stomach clenched in fear. But at the same time, I felt an increase rush of adrenaline go through me, fueling me newfound energy.

Before he reached me, I turned around and ran as fast as I could the other direction, grateful for the burst of energy and all the jogging along the beach I did with Nat on weekends. I should be able to keep going for a good while until I can find an exit. But glancing back, I could see he was right behind me, chasing me with a relentless pace. He seemed determined to get me. And he was quickly catching up.

Kailin Gow

I kept running, and even tried to lose him but he was quick and fast, with reflexes that was highly trained. What was he? I didn't have time to ponder as I tried desperately to pour the last of my energy into a power sprint.

I took off for a while, and then slowed down to almost a crawl. The burst of energy was fleeting and brief. I was almost exhausted and nearing the end of my energy level when those grubby hands wrapped around my neck.

Chapter 13

At moments like these where you were at the mercy of some raving lunatic, you'd pray to God that you'd have sense enough to keep your mouth shut or at least say the right words.

His hands were on my neck, squeezing hard, cutting off my breath, while I struggled to get out. I had only a few seconds left before I would lose consciousness and become brain damaged or dead. I didn't even have the oxygen to spare to talk him out of the situation.

Somewhere in the back of my mind, I remembered what to do. Self-defense classes, karate classes, and even something from watching martial arts movies with Drew and Nat over the years. It was too late for regrets that I didn't equip myself with pepper spray or a stun gun as I had planned earlier. I had to make do with what I had at the moment. I clenched my hands into fists, and pulled forward, trying to slip through the hole I created. No luck, he held on tightly.

I then pull forward and punched him in the ribs with my elbows. He let out a grunt, and loosened his hold on my neck. At that moment, I lifted my foot and stomp as hard as I could down on his foot, which made him drop his hands from my neck. I started coughing, but as sore as my neck was, I had to get away.

Gulping down air into my inflamed lungs, I moved as fast as I could away from him until I was in the dark hallway. Somewhere there was another exit that was accessible. I had dropped my bag near the entrance the first time I tried to get away, but had to leave it. Hopefully it will let whoever happened to show up, know there was someone in the building, and something wasn't quite right.

"Bitch!' the man's voice angrily called out. "I'm going to get you once and for all."

Perfect Summer (Loving Summer #2)

I thought I had made some distance away from him, but I was wrong. The man, who had been stalking Aunt Sookie for years, crept up behind me and grabbed my waist. "No!" I shouted. "Let go!"

"Not until I do what I've dreamt about doing to you once and for all!" he said.

"I'm not Sookie," I said. "I don't even know why you'd waste your time going after me like this."

"You're her daughter," the man said. "You look just like her when she was your age."

"No, I'm not. I'm her niece, but more importantly, I'm not her. She's gone. She's dead. Why go after her?"

"Because," he said. "She was mine."

"You can't own anyone," I said.

"She owned me," Sloane said. "We were about to be married, but she left me, and came to Hollywood. It changed her, turned her into a slut...a harlot, made her sell herself out. All you see of her on television, in the Red Phoenix show, and some films...it wasn't her. She was a sweet small town girl, whose only ambitions in life was to please me, make me breakfast, feed my dogs...then she took an acting class at the local theater, got her guts up to audition for the star role, got it, and then thought she was good enough for Hollywood. She left me as soon as she got a small role in some commercial. Next thing I hear, she's dating people in the biz. Some hotshot actor, then some producer. Had a kid out of wedlock with an actor...she had become morally depraved, and it was my duty to make sure she didn't taint the rest of the world with her lies and sins."

I took a deep breath, thinking through what I was going to say. I had to keep him talking. Sooner or later, Drew will find me. He knew I would be here for the meeting. I just hoped he would figure out the date and time was a set up and try to find me...if only I can get a chance to text him...

"Are you sure that was Aunt Sookie?" I asked. "Are you getting her mixed up with someone else? That biography sounded a lot like Norma Jean Baker's um, Marilyn Monroe's life. Because no one these days, um, no woman of Sookie's age, would go for that taking care of her man's needs, making him breakfast, and feeding his dog shit. You wanted a servant, not a wife."

Great. I should've kept my mouth shut.

I cringed when Sloane threw me an angry look and slapped me. "Watch your mouth, girl," he said. "You don't talk that way to your superiors."

Wow, Sloane was more messed up than I could imagine. The woman he described as Aunt Sookie was someone else I was sure. It was the type of Hollywood rags to riches bio the press machines back in the early days of Hollywood would put together for most of their contracted studio stars. Back then, a role of a woman was so different than today. Aunt Sookie never grew up on a farm, never got engaged to some chauvinist, didn't get knocked up by an actor, and sure did not live in some small town where the only opportunity to act was in the small town theater. This guy was seriously whacked. Putting his fantasy of Sookie in with some Hollywood starlet fantasy of the 1940s.

He wasn't that old, (about thirty-six or so) too, not old enough to have been alive in the 40s, but Nat had said

Sloane was obsessed with comic books and superheroes. Red Phoenix was a comic book super heroine from the 40s.

"Look, I'm sorry Aunt Sookie disappointed you, ran off from your farm and became an actress living in sin," I said. "But she's gone. She's dead. She's repaid all the wrongs she'd inflicted on you. You can't live in the past with her. You have to move on." I paused. "You're young still, and attractive enough...you have a whole life ahead of you. You can find some sweet girl who would want to stay home with you, make you breakfast and feed your dogs, but you can't when you're stuck in the past, only thinking of what happened between you and Aunt Sookie."

Sloane looked like he was chewing over what I just said to him, which made me relaxed a bit. Where was Drew?

"You think I'm attractive," he said, moving his suddenly lust-filled eyes all over my body.

"Attractive to some girl who likes men like you," I said. Boy was that some roundabout answer.

Perfect Summer (Loving Summer #2)

"Well, I'm attracted to you," he said, moving his hand closer until he was lying on top of my thigh. He began moving his hand up and down my thigh. "That first time I saw you at your Aunt's acting school, you were on the ground of the theater, and your dress was up to your stomach, showing off your filthy panties." He shuddered, as though he just climaxed in his pants. "You are a dirty dirty girl. You're just like Sookie, using your beauty to charm men, leading them on, and then dumping them aside." He leaned in, his breath smelling like an ashtray full of rotten eggs and beef jerky. I almost gagged. "I have to cleanse you, make you whole to be good enough to sit at the supper table."

He pushed me down, and tore at my jeans, while fumbling with the button and zipper on his… Oh no! This. Was. Not. Happening. I tried to kick him off, to knee him in the groin, but he was a good hundred pounds larger than me, and had pinned me in place with his body.

"No!" I cried. "I don't want this. You can't force me to have sex with you!"

"Who said we're having sex," he said, reaching into his jeans pocket. "I'm going to brand you with an 'S' for slut."

You mean 'S' for 'Scarlett' as in the Scarlett Letter!

My eyes widen in fear when he pulled out a pocket knife with the sharpest blade.

I tried to head butt him, but he moved his head. Then I tried to find a hold on him to flip him over like in judo, but he seemed to anticipate my every move.

He laughed at my feeble attempt at escaping. "Ex-police officer, now a bodyguard working for a security company known to be celebrity's top pick."

I gulped.

"Donovan Dynamics," Sloan said. "How else did you think I can get some of those photos of you?"

"You...people trust you to protect them..." I was so angry, I raised my hand and slapped him hard.

Did Nat or Drew even knew he worked in their father's company?

Perfect Summer (Loving Summer #2)

His head fell back for a second, before he steadied it to look angrily at me. "For that, missy, you will get fucked, roughly and painfully. I will mess you up so bad that even dogs wouldn't want to stick their dicks into you."

He ripped off my jeans and pulled my underwear down. I wanted to throw up. "No," I said forcefully. "You will not violate my body like that. You do not have my permission."

"No?" he said.

"No! Asshole!" Drew grabbed Sloan's head to punch him while he kicked away his knife.

"Drew!" I sighed, getting up unsteadily.

"Go, run, go to the police," Drew said quickly. "This guy's ex-army. He knows how to fight..."

Sloane's fist slammed against Drew right when he said that, and Drew stumbled back. "Go!" Drew said right before Sloane dragged him up and punched him again.

I turned to go, but I didn't. Drew needed me here. I wasn't some kind of damsel in distress. I could fight. I could help.

I brought out my phone and called 911, telling them the exact location, and even called Nat about Donovan Dynamics' security breach...Sloane.

Then I ran to the nearest emergency fire system, broke the glass, and pulled out the extinguisher. The alarm sounded, sending a signal across campus and to the local fire department that there was a fire at the science building.

I got back in time to see Drew had been beaten, a trickle of blood ran from his mouth. He was being pushed down on his knees by Sloane, and Sloane had taken his pocket knife out and was about to stab Drew in the guts with it. I ran so fast with the extinguisher, pulling out the hose, and sprayed Sloane's face with it until he fell back, dropping the knife.

"Quick, move out of the way," Drew said, taking the extinguisher from me. He brought the extinguisher down hard on Sloane's head once, and then a couple of times more until Sloane's face was a bloody pulp.

I had to stop Drew, pull him back before he killed Sloane.

Perfect Summer (Loving Summer #2)

When the firemen and the police arrived, Drew was still looking shocked and stunned so I told them what happened, and how Drew arrived just in time to defend me against Sloane who had a knife.

They took Sloane away then, and left Drew and I alone to go home. I was going to take Drew to the hospital to get him checked out, but he shook his head "no".

I decided to go back to the Pad with him then. Maybe he just needed a moment to get his adrenaline down and calm down. It was a traumatic experience for all of us. My hands were still shaking as I drove back.

Drew was still in a state of shock when we reached the Pad where I sat him down on the sofa. Somehow, this had really shaken him up, and I sensed something else was going on.

"Drew?" I asked. "What's going on? Are you okay? Everything's taken cared of now, Sloane is with the police. I'm fine. You're fine. You can relax now."

I stroke his back and hugged him tightly, while I murmured how we're both safe and everything will be fine.

When Drew barely responded after ten more minutes, I called Nat to fly out on emergency. Something was seriously wrong.

Drew was not at all normal.

Chapter 14

Nat

I flew out to Malibu in record time. This was one of the highest emergencies classified to use the corporate jet. I didn't have to explain to the crew about the last minute flight at midnight. They all knew, working in a security company, how to act in times of emergencies. Nothing had to be explained.

Normally at this level of an emergency where there has been an attack on one of our own or on a client where attempted murder was involved; I would have to run everything by the head of Donovan Dynamics…my father.

But since he left for a top secret project he was working with the government on a few days ago, he wasn't here to approve it. Instead, it was up to me, when the emergency involved any of the Donovans and/or Summer.

Dad's deal was something I couldn't talk about. In fact, it was so top secret, only a handful of people knew about it – Tom, Peter, Roger, and me. Even mom, Drew, and Rachel didn't know about it. That was intentional. Since it could be very dangerous, the less people knew about it, the less likely this project wouldn't go awry, and people wouldn't get hurt.

It was so dangerous, that even Dad had some doubts whether or not he would be returning back to us alive.

Now I understood the sense of urgency Dad had in trying to get me up to par with the company, having me work there part-time all these years, and now nearly full-time there as one of the executives. Yes, he made me an executive of Donovan Dynamics just last week, the morning of the day I flew out to spend that glorious weekend with Summer. Dad made me acting President of

Donovan Dynamics that day, and I knew something serious was up.

Donovan Dynamics was more than a security company. It was an intelligence company that operated on the highest level of intelligence and operations with the expertise to help countries run their own security and intelligence strategies. Knowing some of the high-level information that Donovan Dynamics was privy too, made Donovan Dynamics powerful and valuable to many organizations and many individuals who could use that knowledge to overrun governments and countries.

With this level of risk involved on a trip like the one my father took, it shouldn't surprise me when I received notice a few hours before I heard from Summer, that my father's party did not make it to their designated place of meeting. Of course the local authorities stated they had tried to find them the best they can, but there was no trace of the party even making it out to their location.

After several calls with the local authorities and government, I felt as though I was being given the run around, not being told the truth, and that there was something they were hiding. Because only a handful of us knew about the secret mission, we decided to use a private mercenary team to track down and bring back my father instead of involving the U.S. government and military.

Because Dad had been missing for a day, and time was of essence, I went ahead and ordered Tom to find some of the top ex-military specialists who were familiar with the country, its culture, and politics, to help us in this mission. I had just finished meeting with them and was told there may be a possibility that I have to go on this mission as well. I had valuable information that my father had entrusted me with that no one else would know, except my father and me. If my father was gone, then I would have to continue with the mission. I had to find out how critical the information I had was to the mission. If I had to go, I'd go. This wasn't a time to be selfish. My father needed me, the company needed me, and apparently our country needed me.

Perfect Summer (Loving Summer #2)

I haven't thought about how I was going to tell Mom and the twins about this. I haven't figured out how I was going to tell Summer about this...just right when everything I've ever wanted with Summer was happening.

But I couldn't even think about our relationship at the moment. The nightmare I always had, about my little brother's condition, may be coming true. I just hope I could be here to help him as much as I could.

****

I got to the Pad as quickly as I could. When I stepped through the door, I was greeted by Summer with an enormous hug and a kiss. God, even now, just the sight of her and the feel of her in my arms could give me an instant hard-on. If I wasn't so worried about Drew as I was now, I would be tearing off Summer's little tank top, unbuttoning her shorts, and comforting her in the best way possible.

But I was here to see if Drew and Summer was alright. And I was here to be with Summer. What she must've experienced with that asshole Sloane, made me want to seek him out and make sure he never see the light of day again.

"Summer," I pulled her into my arms and held her so tight, I could hear her gasp. I loosen my grip, but buried my face into her chest."I'm so sorry I wasn't there to keep you safe." The reality of what could've happened if Drew wasn't there to save her from Sloane again, hit me. "I could've lost you, Summer," I whispered hoarsely into her chest and hair. Oh God, this time could've ended in tragedy.

"Nat," Summer said lightly. "I'm okay. I'm fine." She lifted my face to look at me before placing her soft lips on mine. As if we were on fire, we kissed with a passion that contained all the fears, hurt, and love we felt in the last few hours. We broke apart when we heard a clanging of pots and pans in the kitchen.

Summer looked more surprised than I did. "That's Drew!" She took my hand and pulled me into the living room into the kitchen.

"Drew!" she cried out, rushing over to him and wrapping her arms around him tightly. "Oh God, Drew, I was so scared with the way you were acting." She kissed him on the lips and brushed his hair back from his face with both of her hands.

For a moment, I was struck with jealousy when I saw the look of love cross her face as she gazed tenderly at Drew.

"How are you feeling, Drew?" she asked him. "Do you want to talk about it?"

Drew was looking down at her, his arms wrapped around her, one hand caressing her face with one thumb rubbing her cheek. "I…I wanted to kill him," he said. "I would have if you didn't stop me." He bent down to kiss Summer briefly, and hugged her tight. "I couldn't stop myself, but he was going to kill you, and I wanted to stop him for once and forever."

I went up to Drew and Summer, and hugged both of them. Drew looked startled to see me, and stiffen, dropping his arms from Summer's waist.

"Nat!" he said. "I didn't know you're here."

"Yeah, uh, It's good to see you're alright, Bro," I said giving him a pat on his arm. "I tried to get here as soon as I could, but had a meeting I couldn't miss."

Summer came over to me and rubbed my arm, "But you're here now," she said. "That's what's important, and Drew's fine now."

I looked over at Drew and Summer. "If I wasn't mistaken, it seems as though Drew's fine here." I looked at Summer, "Why did you think something was seriously wrong with him...besides being a smartass bastard," I joked.

Summer blushed. "I didn't think anything was wrong at first, Nat, but honestly Drew, you had me worried. You seemed completely out of it, in shocked, for a good hour or so."

Drew shook his head. "I just kinda zoned out, that's all. Never felt like it before, but I guessed all those intense emotions and my adrenaline going like that, was too much for a while, and I shut down." He grabbed Summer and enfolded her in his arms. "I'm sorry I scared you, Sum." He tweaked her nose, "I promise to try not to veg out on you again."

Summer smiled the smile that could melt any guy's heart. "That's okay, Drew. You saved my life today, I think I can forgive you for that."

Drew smiled back at her. As jealous as I was watching the love flowing between them, I couldn't help thinking how happy Drew looked just now, just holding Summer.

Dammit, part of me thought they looked so sweet together, yet another part of me wanted to rip Summer out of his arms and claim her as mine. If the guy Summer was looking at with that adoring look she also gave me, wasn't my little brother, I think I would've lost it.

But I wasn't the one who saved Summer from Sloane the first time he attacked her at the Academy. Drew did. And I wasn't the one who saved her again just now. Drew did.

My brother was a true hero, and any girl who he saved from a maniac like Sloane would be completely in love with Drew now.

Kailin Gow

And Drew...my poor brother, must've been really affected by this experience with Sloane to have zoned out. He looked fine just now talking to Summer and me, but I knew why he zoned out...I had Mom's doctor's report with me along with some pills. I was afraid I would have to give them to Drew to get him out of the state he was in. Thank goodness he came out of it without having to use the pills, but I brought it just in case.

I have to let Drew know. It was his life, and I can't protect him with this knowledge any longer. He had to protect himself and arm himself with as much knowledge as he could in order to fight it and lead a normal life as best as he could.

I had to tell Drew, he could be bi-polar like Mom.

I'll have to let Summer know the possibility that all of us Donovan kids may have some form of mental illness.

I didn't have time to worry about protecting anyone from this anymore. I have to find my father and do whatever it takes to get him back and to save the company.

I checked my voicemail for the message I've been dreading hearing all night long.

About the whereabouts of my father.

It was there…one single message that would change everything.

Voicemail: Nat, your father is alive. We're sending the mercenary team we hired to find him and bring him back alive at any cost. We tried to think of a way you would not have to physically go to the area of the situation, but we need leverage to get your father out alive. We depart for Afghanistan tomorrow night. Be at the hangar then.

Chapter 15

<u>Summer</u>

Nat and Drew spent a lot of time talking and hanging with each other that night at the Pad. It was like old times…like good times especially the time the Donovans were here with me the last summer Aunt Sookie was alive.

We all played video games like Pac Man and Asteroids…games that we played as children, which were from Aunt Sookie's own private collection. Nat and Drew even worked together in the kitchen, whipping up a delicious meal for dinner.

Perfect Summer (Loving Summer #2)

Towards the end of the night, we decided to go for a midnight jog and swim.

All three of us got dressed in jogging outfits and ran as a group along the beach, passing by our favorite childhood haunts along the way and laughing about how we thought the caves we've seen were really Count Dracula's lair or Batman's cave. As we jogged, we retold stories Aunt Sookie told us about castles and knights, dragons, and ogres…about fantastic fantasies with epic proportions, about the fey folk who lived in Feyland with the magic to cure all sickness.

We ran for a while and decided to head back for a quick dip in the pool.

Of course, the two men I was undeniably and unbelievably hot for were already there in their boxer shorts, swimming, dipping each other into the water, and rough-housing it like when they were thirteen when I returned from changing into a bikini. It was a daring but cute number, a pale pink string bikini with a cute ruffled bottom. Daring because the top barely covered my breasts.

The boys stopped playing to glance over at me. Both looking sinfully dark and aroused as they openly gave me the once over. Drew was the first to say something.

"Summer, you look incredible," he said, getting out of the pool and coming over to me, his boxer shorts wet against his body. The sight of his muscles, perfect v, and manhood dripping wet near me, made me want to grab him and kiss the living daylights out of him. Pulling me to him, he bent down , as if he was going to kiss me on the lips, but kissed the top of my head instead. He gave me a wicked smile and said, "I have to take off for an early morning football practice session with the team tomorrow. I'll see you soon."

I hugged him tightly then and said, "Thank you for saving me, Drew. You deserve the hero award today."

"Thank you," Drew smiled. "I think you do, too. You're as much of a hero as I am."

"We saved each other," I said smiling. "You sure you don't want to stay?"

"No, I'm alright," Drew said. "Nat'll be here, and I know you two would want to spend some time together."

I raised my eyebrows. "But you're welcome to stay, too."

"No," Drew said, looking pained and sad. "Nat has a lot of things he need to tell you, Summer. It's better I don't stay. You'll want to spend some time with him, Summer. And for the first time in my life, Summer, I'm Team Nat."

With that, he walked into his room and within minutes, came out fully dressed. He glanced at me with the warmest eyes, but darted them to an area behind me.

Nat had gotten out of the pool, and was standing behind me, semi-wet. He had the sense to grab a towel and began toweling himself off. When dried, he wrapped the towel around his waist low emphasizing his v in the most sexiest way.

Drew went up to Nat and gave him a strong man-hug. "I'll see you before you take off, Nat." He hugged Nat again and left.

*****

As soon as Drew left, I turned to Nat, who had moved into stand behind me, wrapping his arms around my waist and kissing my shoulders.

"You look like a treat," Nat said, "Pale pink suits you."

"Seducing me isn't going to keep me from asking...did you have something you needed to talk to me about?"

Nat grinned sheepishly. "Well...I was hoping we'd get to bed first and worry about that later."

"Depends on what you have to talk to me about," I said.

"Ok," Nat said, "But it was such a perfect night tonight...I don't want to spoil it yet."

"But Drew knows, right?" I said. "Why shouldn't I?"

"No, I was planning on telling you, Summer. But I want to savour this moment and us like this as long as I could."

I was beginning to worry now. "Nat, does this have to do with your mother or Drew?"

"Kinda, but there's more...let's sit down."

He took my hands and led me to the sofa, where I sat next to him, anticipating what he was going to say.

"There are a couple of things, Summer, and I haven't told you about them because they're really not for me to tell. But circumstances have made it so that you have to know. Then you can decide if you wanted to help us out or not."

I looked deep into Nat's eyes and said, "I'm part of the Donovans, Nat. There isn't any family I want to be part of more than yours, as crazy as it seems, and there isn't anywhere else I'd rather be, than with you." I kissed him soundly on the lips, and rubbed his hands in mine. I knew how hard it was for Nat or any of the Donovans to open up so for Nat to say he wanted me to be privileged to what he was going to say, outside of family, I felt somehow honored. I kissed him again, "I love you, Nat Donovan." I kissed him again, "So. Incredibly. Much."

Nat kissed me back, and held me tight against him. "Gosh, Summer, this is harder than I thought it would be, but I need to, I have to do this. There is so much at stake that I have to put aside my own dreams and wants right now…which is to always be with you."

I stopped kissing him, and pulled back. "What are you talking about?"

"Sum," Nat said, "What I'm about to tell you has to be of strictest confidence. Lives arc at stake and everything can be jeopardized if this isn't kept secret. No kidding. But, I have to go on an important trip to Afghanistan. My dad's been missing for a couple of days on a trip he went on for Donovan Dynamics. Only a handful of people know about this trip, not even my mother, Drew or Rachel knows about it. I found out yesterday that they located him, and he's alive, but I'll have to go as leverage to get him out. It's very dangerous, and I…don't want to leave everything here as it is…"

Nat broke off, and he looked sad, but determined. "Mom is getting better. I found her a new doctor, but I think Drew may have a bit of what Mom has…"

He paused, and he watched my face closely for my reaction.

"What do you think he has, Nat?" I asked.

"He may be a bit bipolar," Nat said. "His personalities and social interactions may be affected."

My mouth dropped open. It explained how Drew could act hot and cold to me within a short span of time. It also explained how he reacted to Sloane, yesterday. "Do you know, for sure?"

"No, it's very mild if he has it, but sometimes, it shows up…like yesterday, I think." Nat looked straight ahead and said, "I mean anyone would be shaken up by what happened, especially you, Summer. You should be shaken and almost traumatized. I know a lot of girls would be, after being nearly raped and killed by this stalker twice. And all the mindfucking games played on you. But you've proven to be stronger than all that. You're amazing,

Summer, and I don't mean that because I love you, but because it's the truth."

I looked at Nat, and then I couldn't help it...tears formed in my eyes. "I'm not so strong as you think, Nat. I know I'm going to miss you like crazy when you're in Afghanistan. I'll be worried the entire time, but I don't want you to worry about me, too."

Nat reached over and held me. "I promise to be as careful as I could. I won't be reckless, and I intend to return to you safe and sound. My father may not be the best husband in the world, but he's smart enough to get to where he is. He's put together a sharp team of people who know what they're doing. I'm in good hands...but I just don't know when I'll be back."

"Whatever happens, Nat," I said, "don't worry about things at home. I'll help Drew and Rachel out. I'll even help things out with your mother and Donovan Dynamics. Just let me know what I have to do..."

Nat kissed me then and said, "I'll leave you a note of instructions then. On your dressing table. Don't read it until you're ready…I told Drew about everything last night, and he took it surprisingly well. I'm going to count on him and you to stand in for me at Donovan Dynamics and at home while I'm gone…"

"I will," I said. "I promise."

Nat searched my face for a second before kissing me. "I love you so much, Sum. I always have…I'm going to miss you, this…"

I gulped down my tears and pushed Nat down. I grabbed hold of his boxers and slid them down his legs. "Then let's make the most of the time we have together."

I bent my head down towards Nat's hard abs, kissed it, and made my way down.

*****

That night, we made love with an intensity and an intimacy that was higher than we've experienced. Knowing how he had to go to Afghanistan and how he'd been keeping his father's secret, made me want to hold unto him forever and love the hurt right out of him.

In the heat of passion, I told him he will always be my first of everything, that I will always love him no matter how far apart we are. I meant it, too. It became clear to me that Nat had always been the one I loved.

The next day, after having breakfast with Nat, I was sore all over. I had suffered some cuts and bruises from Sloane's attack on me, but it was replaced by the delicious soreness of Nat's passionate lovemaking. I couldn't get enough of him, and he couldn't get enough from me.

"Summer," he said, kissing me as he gathered his things to go. "I don't know when I'll be back from Afghanistan. I hope this mission would be quick and over with soon, but there are no guarantees. What happened with Drew...can you help watch him for me, make sure he's okay? And Rachel...she actually looks up to you and admire you...if she gets too out-of-hand, not the Rachel kind, but if she flips out too much about things..."

I smiled gently. "Don't worry Nat, I will watch out for Drew and Rachel. How could I not? I love them, too..."

Perfect Summer (Loving Summer #2)

"Drew's going to be taking over a lot of my duties when I'm away, Summer, especially with Mom and Donovan Dynamics...I just hope it's not too much. He thinks he could do it all, but he's only human. With Drew and Rachel...having a possibility of what Mom has, I just wanted to make sure someone stable and strong, like you - mentally strong, can step in when they need you. You've always been there for me, Summer, and I can't thank you enough for that. But mostly," he kissed me hard, "it just makes me love you more each day."

Then he left.

Chapter 16

Drew

a week later

Nat is missing. He was supposed to come back today, but didn't make it back. The mission was more dangerous than we had originally thought, and I'm besides myself with guilt, thinking I should have persuaded Nat not to go. It was one thing to lose Dad, but now Nat? As much as I teased Nat for being the responsible one in the family, he really was the glue to hold everything and everyone together. Growing up, being stupid kid like I was, I couldn't appreciate that kind of dedication and self-sacrifice for the family. Neither did Rachel.

While Rachel and I played and went on our way to do our own things, pursue our own dreams, Nat set aside his own dreams, his own wishes to follow along the family business and to take care of Mom. He was the real man in the family, while I was just some kid.

No wonder why Summer looked up to him so much and loved him with that constant hard crush. From the start, even at a young age, Summer recognized and reached out for the love of a responsible man who could one day be her equal, fulfill her potential, and help complete her. She saw that in Nat. Unlike the other girls, who just wanted to have fun in the now, Summer already knew she wanted someone like Nat as her anchor. I

But now he was missing and perhaps gone.

I can't bear to think of it. But I have no choice. I have to step up and be the grown up and step into Nat's shoes.

*****

Mom still thinks Dad and Nat are on a business trip to the Caribbeans, because Rachel and I didn't want to upset her and cause her to fall further into depression. I don't know how long before she finds out but now Rachel knows about Nat. She knows about the possibility of us Donovan kids having what Mom has. It's brought Rachel and I closer, and despite how she flew off and broke down crying when she heard about Dad and Nat, she was still strong enough to comfort me. I guessed being twins, despite being fraternal twins, we were able to sense when one was hurt so at least I had Rachel to rely on...and Summer.

*****

What to do about Summer?

Even without trying unlike those girls who are all over me in the front row of Standish's class, Summer managed to blow them out of the water as the hottest and classiest girl in class.

They're easy. Not like Summer. She's not loose, she's not easy, but she was sexy enough to make a man want her constantly and to forget everyone else.

It was easier being able to keep from ravishing her every chance I got with Nat physically being here or nearby. But now he was missing, and I have to step into his shoes to help run Donovan Dynamics, to make sure Summer is safe, and to be her shining knight in armor and her hero.

With her crying like this, looking so vulnerable and sweet in my arms, with her smelling like a bright new day, and her eyes imploring sweetly at me to kiss her, to make things alright, and to make love to her; it was too hard to resist. I wanted to comfort her to tell her all will be fine, but I didn't know if it would myself. All I knew was that the best way to comfort her was to give her what she wanted, what she craved from me. I knew she was missing Nat and his touch. I knew she was waiting for him to return, and things would go back to normal, but he wasn't here, and there was no telling when. And if.

Fuck. Please God do not let Nat and my father die, I prayed.

As much as I wanted Summer, I didn't want to have her because Nat died. I wanted her to love me for me, not as a substitute for Nat.

I've never seen Summer so distraught as she was. Not even when Aunt Sookie died. She really did love Nat. I knew that now.

"Drew," she cried. "I keep praying and hoping it's not true," she said. "Nat can't have disappeared. He can't have gone missing. He assured me he wouldn't leave me, that he would return, and everything would be alright." She paused, sobs racking her body until she could barely breathe. "I loved him so much. I craved him so much. I'm having withdrawals. I can't. I can't imagine not being able to ever touch him again!"

She sobbed so much and didn't eat all day that I finally pulled her into my arms. All the resolve I've had these past weeks dissolved. How can I fight this longing for her? I must be crazy sick in love with her beyond reason. For even when I watched Nat make love to her, kissed and devour her breasts while stroking her core with his fingers; I was so turned on, I almost came just standing there, marveling how beautiful Summer looked with her face alive with passionate ecstasy. What kind of a sick bastard got turned on watching his brother make love to the girl he was in love with? A sick one, some kind of perv, that's who. But I've reached a point of surrender, not caring what anyone thought of me, only caring about this incredible impossible passion between Summer and I.

My mouth crashes on hers like an uncontrollable tidal wave, and we kiss each other like starved animals. My tongue forces her mouth to open wider and I delve in.

I can still control myself I tell myself, and I pull back, scrambling to keep at a distance, but she pulls me in, grabbing hold of my hair and my face with both hands. She's holding my face in place while she tenderly kiss my lips from the top lip to the bottom in small kisses that ended up with her planting her lips open mouth against mine. It is the most loving, sweetest, yet sexy kiss of dance I've ever had. But when her soft pink tongue dart out to trace my lips and then to brush against mine, I knew there was no going back. There can never be a go-back with her. She had claimed me the moment we first kissed.

I. Am. So. Fucked.

Epilogue

<u>Summer</u>

I'm in a state of oblivion. I could not even function. For days after hearing about Nat, I became catatonic. It was worse than when I heard about Aunt Sookie. I somehow had time to prepare for the news of her death, knowing she was bad off at the hospital. But Nat...

My heart feels as though it has been ripped out.

For once, I didn't know what to do.

Nat had always been my rock, even if he was in San Francisco, even if he didn't know it. He had always been my mental rock. Now he was gone.

The only solace I had was with Drew and Rachel. I didn't care anymore about the boundaries I had with Drew. Friends, lover, non-friend...it didn't matter to me anymore. I just knew I felt so much for him, and he was here. He was here for me, and I was here for him.

It hit Drew hard about Nat, too.

So in a way...we comforted each other the best and only way we knew how...with each other.

Then one day when the pain subsided a bit, I remembered Nat's instructions to me, instructions he left for me about Donovan Dynamics.

I went to my room and found the beautiful linen envelope on top of my dressing table, addressed to: Summer. And carefully brought it to the kitchen counter, where I had shared many breakfasts throughout the years with Nat. I gingerly opened it, and began reading it.

Nat's Letter to Summer

My Perfect Summer,

I know we're used to calling or texting each other whenever we needed to talk to each other, but I wanted to try something different this time, because this is one of those times that I wish to preserve in memory, as well as paper in hopes that someday our children or future generation could read and cherish.

Aunt Sookie had always been fond of letters, written in the old fashioned way. That when forced to sit down to write a letter, taking pen to paper, you spend more time thinking about what you want to say, and how to say it.

She told me once that traditions like that are worth preserving. And when it comes to anything to do with you, I want to make sure it is preserved.

Kailin Gow

Aunt Sookie lived life to the fullest. She taught us to learn from the past, enjoy the now, and prepare for the future. You have always been part of my past, my now, and even my future.

I have avoided love for so long. I have been too afraid to open myself up to it, afraid I will only be disappointed. But when you came along into my life, so new to the world at only four years old to my five years old, I felt the stirring of love and friendship. It wasn't until we were beginning our teens that the love I felt for you was the kind a man has for a woman.

My instructions to you when you're ready to read this letter is to live life to the fullest. To love life to the fullest. Regardless of who you end up with, who is blessed to be the man to spend the rest of your life with, I wish you happiness. And a lifetime of lasting love.

Perfect Summer (Loving Summer #2)

Wherever you go, whatever the weather and time of year; with you, it'll always be a Perfect Summer.

I love you with all my heart.

Your Nat in Shining Armor

Kailin Gow

Summer, Drew, Nat, Rachel, and Astor's story continues in

Book 2 of the Donovan Brothers Series and Book 3 of the
Loving Summer Series

Secrets of the Fall (Donovan Brothers Book #2)

June 2013

Lasting Summer (Loving Summer Series #3)

October 2013

The Truth Behind LOVING SUMMER

After Loving Summer was published, I received many emails asking me if it was based on a true story.

Loving Summer is a compilation of 2 families I knew growing up. Ironically, two families with two gorgeous brothers and a pretty sister.

Both of them were families my family grew close to at the time their mothers were having difficulties. Neither of them knew of each other, but both at different periods in their lives went through similar situations of divorce and being a single mother raising three kids.

The character I most resembled is Aunt Sookie. Mainly because I have or rather had diabetes like the kind Aunt Sookie had. Complicated and potentially life threatening. For a moment in 2012, I did face a life and death situation with my health, brought on by diabetes.
With the love of my family and the strength from prayers, and a dedicated lifestyle change of healthier

Kailin Gow

living and choices, I was able to get to a point of normalcy, getting to a diagnosis of "Normal".

Loving Summer is a miracle book, and if it wasn't for that book and the situation that coincidentally came up in it, I would not have been able to be diagnosed and "cured" of diabetes.

Sometimes writing is a way of growth and journey for an author as well as a form of entertainment for readers. I am humbly and sincerely grateful for the opportunity for Loving Summer and my books to touch you in any way.
Thank you for reading Loving Summer. I hope you enjoyed it.

If you enjoyed it, I appreciate you letting others know. Positive reviews and word-of-mouth is very much appreciated, too.

Feedback, comments, etc! You can reach me at:

kailingowbooks@aol.com

Perfect Summer (Loving Summer #2)

Books Mentioned in Loving Summer

The FADE Series

Book 1: FADE

A Thriller from Bestselling Author Kailin Gow

What if you found out you never existed?

My name is Celestra Caine. I am seventeen years old, which makes me a senior at Richmond High. I never thought this would happen to me, but it has... I'm one of those people you see every day, go to school with, remember seeing at the supermarket or the mall, and then one day you don't hear about them any longer. They're gone, and eventually, you forget them.

Book 2: Falling

What is Celestra Caine? Who is she and did she ever existed? The Faders and the Others clash at the Underground, sending everything into a tailspin. Celestra is pulled into more intrigue, more danger, and more romance, as she discovers who she is and why everyone wants to get her.

Book 3: Forgotten

Perfect Summer (Loving Summer #2)

A love that can never be forgotten…

The truth about Celestra Caine comes back in the most shocking way. Everyone knew Celestra Caine was dangerous, but they didn't know she was THAT dangerous… As Celestra's memories begin returning to her after being Faded, and her identity is revealed, she learns the fate of the world really is in her hands, and that she, the mysterious and sexy fader Jack, and her handsome ex-boyfriend Gray are more connected to each other than she ever imagined.

In this dystopian YA thriller, where nothing is what it

seems, sometimes love can be strong enough to withstand time and space and never be forgotten.

Book 4: Fever

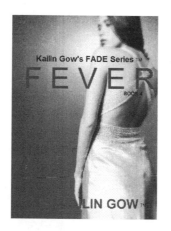

Who had survived the Apocalypse?

In Fever, the fourth book in Kailin Gow's FADE dystopian thriller series, Celes' memories return with a vengeance.

Jack's memories are aligned with hers, and together they

embark on fulfilling the mission they had set themselves to accomplished in their past.

Visit Kailin Gow's Amazon Store for More Books and more Heart-stopping Romances and Compelling Stories

http://www.amazon.com/Kailin-Gow/e/B002BMAEH4/ref=ntt_athr_dp_pel_1

Kailin Gow

The Protégé

For mature readers age 18 and up due to sexual situations

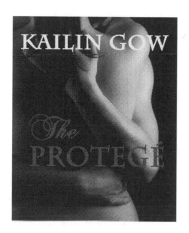

When worldly and sexy famed music composer Sebastian
Sorensen took on sweet and innocent Serena Singleton as
his Protege, he took on more than he bargained for.

Meet Sebastian Sorensen - famed Hollywood music

composer, university professor, and producer. Sexy, intelligent, talented, and insatiable. He loves a good challenge.

Meet Serena Singleton - young up-and-coming talent, who is as sweet and innocent as Sebastian Sorensen is worldly and darkly damaged. As soon as she walked into his office, disheveled, late, and in need of guidance (as well as a good spanking), she became his challenge.

As their world collide amidst dinner dates, foul play, and intrigue; the more they learn of each other, the more they want, until the lines are blurred. Who is the Protege and who is the Master?

Kailin Gow

Weigh in on LOVING SUMMER!

Which Team are You On? Who should Summer End Up With? Weigh in and Help the author decide:

Team Drew

Team Nat

Team Astor

Vote on theEDGEbooks.com's

Loving Summer Poll

Find Out What Happens to Nat, Drew, and Summer in the Upcoming Donovan Brothers Book:

Secrets of the Fall (Donovan Brothers #2)

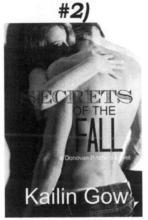

The Donovan Brothers... two gorgeous brothers in love with the same girl. How far would they fall to have her? One of them will claim her, but the other will find her. Only one can win her forever, unless their family secrets destroy everything.

Kailin Gow

OTHER BOOKS FROM KAILIN GOW

The FROST Series

The PULSE Series

Wicked Woods Series

Desire Series

Steampunk Scarlett Series

The Fire Wars Series

Fade Series

Circus of Curiosities

You & Me Trilogy

Never Say Never Series

Alchemists Academy Series

Wordwick Games Series

Phantom Diaries Series

Perfect Summer (Loving Summer #2)

Beautiful Beings Series

Stoker Sisters Series

And More!

VISIT KAILIN'S WEBSITE to learn about new releases, the most awesome contests and parties, what Kailin and friends are doing in the community, workshops and events Kailin will be at and more at:

http://www.kailingow.com

http://kailingow.wordpress.com

and

on Twitter at: @kailingow

Kailin Gow

KAILIN GOW'S 18+ Adult Romance Books Newsletter

Are you over 18? Would you like to know more about Kailin's books for adults and new adults?

Sign up for her newsletter at:

kailingowbook(at)aol(dot)com

Thank you for reading! – Kailin